Goldclimbers

Novels by Nancy Luenn

Arctic Unicorn
Goldclimbers

Goldclimbers

N A N C Y L U E N N

ATHENEUM 1991 NEW YORK

COLLIER MACMILLAN CANADA
TORONTO
MAXWELL MACMILLAN INTERNATIONAL PUBLISHING GROUP
NEW YORK OXFORD SINGAPORE SYDNEY

Thanks to Betty Swift, John Marshall and his students
at the University of Washington metalworking lab,
and to Charles Pearson

Atheneum
Macmillan Publishing Company
866 Third Avenue
New York, NY 10022

Collier Macmillan Canada, Inc.
1200 Eglinton Avenue East
Suite 200
Don Mills, Ontario M3C 3N1

First edition
Printed in the United States of America
1 2 3 4 5 6 7 8 9 10
Designed by Kimberly M. Hauck
Bird motif drawn by Stephen Marchesi

Library of Congress Cataloging-in-Publication Data

Luenn, Nancy.
Goldclimbers/by Nancy Luenn.—1st ed.
p.   cm.
*Summary: Living in a community that creates objects in gold,
fifteen-year-old Aracco knows he doesn't want to be a master
goldsmith like his father but sees no other future for himself until,
when the supply of gold is threatened, he is selected to find
a way to a legendary city whose streets are paved with gold.*
ISBN 0-689-31585-6
[1. Gold—Fiction. 2. Fantasy.] I. Title.
PZ7.L9766Go 1991
[Fic]—dc20   90-589   CIP   AC

To my brother Kenneth

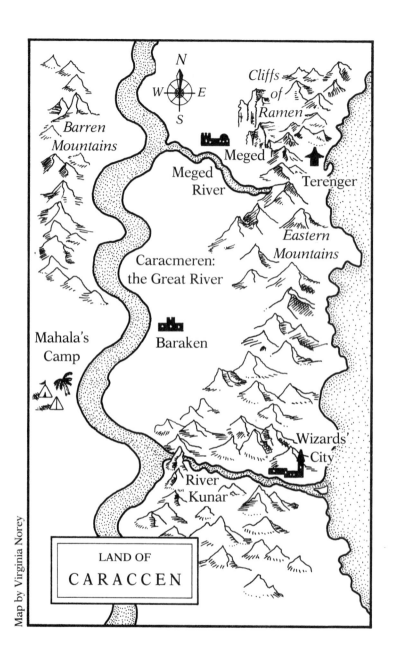

Barren
Mountains

Cliffs
of
Ramen

Meged
River

Meged

Terenger

Eastern
Mountains

Caracmeren:
the Great River

Mahala's
Camp

Baraken

Wizards'
City

River
Kunar

LAND OF
CARACCEN

Goldclimbers

Aracco pushed down the handle of the bellows and watched flames leap around the crucibles planted in the coals. He let the bellows rise, then forced them down again. His dark brown hands matched the color of the wooden handle. The fierce heat beat against his face and sweat beaded on his forehead. Inside the crucibles, gold nuggets melted slowly, dissolving into bright, hot liquid.

Of all the apprentice tasks, he hated working the bellows most. He disliked watching the metal lose its shape, liked it better as the rough lumps he sometimes found on the abandoned goldcliff. He would rather be hauling water to the cooling troughs, or pounding ingots into sheet gold, or even polishing the finished goldwork. Better than endlessly pushing breath into the forging fire.

He wished he was climbing in the abandoned gold

quarry instead. In the smithy he felt cramped and restless. All around him rang the clangor of many hammers striking gold. The noise resounded inside him until he thought he would burst.

A smith lifted the stone crucibles from the fire and set three more in their places. Aracco pumped the leather bellows, thinking about climbing—climbing for gold. But how could he, a goldsmith's only son, ever hope to be a climber? He longed to win his father's praise. So how could he tell him that he did not want to be a smith? His hands clenched tighter on the bellows, and he forced air through them until the fire roared. Inside the crucibles, the edges of the unforged gold began to blur.

"Aracco!" At the sound of his best friend's voice, Aracco turned.

Valaren stood near the hearth. He was the color of red-brown earth, from his tangled hair to his clay-splattered boots. He'd been polishing goldwork with powdered clay since noon, not sweating at the fire. Aracco scowled, wishing he stood in Valaren's place. His friend seemed at home in the smithy, as much a part of it as the earthen floor. And he had an ease with words that Aracco envied.

If I had his gift, Aracco brooded, *I could tell my father how I feel.* But he felt speechless even at the thought of it.

Valaren gave him a mischievous smile and gestured toward the open door. "Let's go climbing!" he yelled above the din in the smithy. "I've gotten leave—for both of us!"

2

Aracco's mood cleared. Stepping back from the bellows, he signaled to one of the younger apprentices. "Quick!" Aracco shouted. "Before the mastersmith thinks better of it."

He waited impatiently for the other boy to take his place, then ducked out the back door of the smithy, hard upon Valaren's heels. The apprentices went climbing whenever they could, the older boys teaching the younger ones. It gave them a time all their own, away from the critical eyes of their masters.

Outside, the quiet in the alley that lay between the smithy and the guildhall set Aracco's ears ringing. Afternoon sunlight blazed off the whitewashed walls. A summer breeze swirled the dust, cooling his sweat-soaked tunic and finding its way through his springy black hair. Glad to be out of the smithy, Aracco grinned up at his friend. "Good work, Valaren!"

Valaren smiled, his eyes bright with mischief. He was the only apprentice who could wheedle free time from the mastersmith. "I know you hate the bellows," he said. "And it's a great day for climbing."

They turned onto the herders' road leading out of the village toward the high mountain pastures. Valaren had been his constant friend since they were first apprenticed. Although Aracco's skin was several shades darker, Valaren had never taunted him about his kinship with the desert tribes. Not like Nago, the mastersmith's son.

At the thought of Nago, Aracco spat into the dust. They had been enemies for years. Nago bullied the younger boys and flaunted his status as mastersmith's son. Aracco defended the others when he could and settled his own disputes with Nago with his fists. But he sometimes wished an eiroc would come and carry off the bully.

Shoving Nago and the smithy from his mind, Aracco tried to match tall Valaren's longer stride. The road wound through dry foothills, following the course of the Meged River. As they left the village, a jagged line of peaks beyond the foothills thrust into the sky.

"Look, Aracco!" They paused, staring up together at the eastern mountains.

There must be routes up there that have never been climbed, Aracco thought, and said aloud, "I wish I was a climber!"

Valaren glanced at him. "You sound like Gemmel," he said. "There's little adventure in being a gold-climber's apprentice."

"But when I finished my apprenticeship and became a climber—" Aracco stopped, unsure how to explain the lure of it. Roaming where he pleased all winter long and then, when summer came again, the challenge of the cliffs. He picked up a stone and hurled it toward the mountains. "I've far less chance of being a goldclimber than Gemmel."

Saying it aloud, he felt as if the smithy walls were lowering around him like the bars of a cage. When Gemmel's apprenticeship at the smithy was finished, the younger boy would be free to choose the cliffs.

But his *father is not the finest smith in Meged,*

thought Aracco. He knew that his own father's passion for gold was considered a great gift, had often heard it whispered in the village circle.

Everyone expects me to follow in my father's path. What would the villagers say if I chose to leave the guild? He could almost hear their voices, swarming around him like angry wasps. And even worse would be the disappointment in his father's eyes. His father had never criticized flaws in the goldwork Aracco brought home. But Aracco knew he could see the mark of every awkward hammer blow, and his father's silent judgment rankled more than if he had spoken. Turning from his unpleasant thoughts, he fixed his gaze on the mountains. With his mind, he traced one of the high ridges, and his eyes ascended to the summit.

"Beyond them lies Terenger," Valaren murmured, "with its streets of gold. I would like to find a way there."

"And I would like to climb those cliffs," said Aracco. Staring up at them, he felt he could almost touch the cool, unquarried stone.

"Are you a wizard then, that you can charm eirocs?" teased Valaren.

Aracco shuddered. Eirocs were giant birds of prey, larger than a man, that lived among the mountain cliffs. Although climbers had tried to cross the eastern mountains, seeking Terenger, no one had returned. And so the legend of its golden streets remained unproven.

"Do you think the streets are really gold?" asked Aracco.

"Yes," replied Valaren. "But even if they are not, I would still wish to see Terenger."

Aracco gazed at the tallest peaks, sharing his friend's longing for adventure. *Valaren might find a way,* he thought, *and even gain our master's leave. But I . . .* He scowled at the horizon. *I've no skill with words and little more with gold. I should be in the smithy if I ever hope to win my father's praise. But I would rather go climbing!* He shook off his thoughts impatiently and hurried up the road, keeping pace with Valaren.

About half a league from the village, the road bridged a steep-walled ravine. Once, the ravine had been quarried by the climbers' guild. Now only the smiths' apprentices of Meged scaled the walls of the abandoned goldcliff. Despite the danger, the mastersmith permitted them to climb. Climbing strengthened the bond of the guild, setting them apart from the other village boys. And it made them respect the craft of the climbers. This was vital, because the guild at Meged would be nothing without their gold.

Turning aside before the bridge, Aracco and Valaren followed a faded track that curved away from the herders' road. The track descended steeply into the quarry. They scrambled down the path, sending loose stones clattering down the wall of the ravine. At this time of year, the creek that had carved the ravine was dry, leaving only patches of wet sand between the scattered boulders in its rocky bed.

Aracco leaped from boulder to boulder, his spirits lifting as they neared the goldcliff. Already he could imagine the feel of rough stone beneath his fingers. He settled at last on a large flat rock and turned to gaze up at the cliff.

The goldclimbers had gouged deep furrows in the face of the cliff, following the horizontal bands of gold. When the veins were quarried to the depth permitted by the climbers' guild, the ravine had been deserted for richer cliffs northeast of Meged. Although the pebbled bands of goldbearing rock were now empty troughs of shadow, the apprentices sometimes found gold nuggets in the crevices.

The mined routes up the cliff were easy climbs, with deeply cut footholds. Aracco turned his attention to the rock that had carried no gold. There was a new route he wanted to climb.

"I'm going to try the Beak," he told Valaren, gesturing toward a pinnacle of rock jutting into the sky like the beak of a bird. His heart beat faster as he said it. No apprentice had tried to climb the Beak since the day, seven years ago, that Gemmel's eldest brother had fallen to his death.

"Are you sure?" said Valaren, his voice uncertain. "Shall I set a topline?" He nodded toward the cache where they kept their climbing ropes and irons. Aracco shook his head. Why dull the challenge?

"I'll climb better without it." Although their elders would forbid it if they knew, the older boys often climbed unroped.

Aracco studied the Beak. The yellow cliff below it

soared straight up, then curved outward, forming the sharp-edged spire they called the Beak. He climbed it with his eyes, his muscles tensing with anticipation. He had thought many times of climbing it. Now he felt ready.

He jumped off the flat boulder, his fingers itching to begin. Then he paused, looking anxiously over his shoulder at his friend. "Are you climbing with me?"

If Valaren said yes, he would set a topline. Valaren did not have the skill to climb the Beak unroped. He waited, impatient, hoping he would say no.

His friend gestured with feigned laziness toward the quarried part of the cliff. "I'll leave the route-finding to you. Meet you at the top."

Aracco grinned, relieved. Valaren didn't seem to care that Aracco, one year younger, was the better climber.

Aracco approached the cliff, his eyes tracing the way he would climb. He reached up for the first hold, his hand tightening on the stone. He swung one leg up and found his footing. His leg muscles tensed, bringing the other foot up to a tiny toehold. He reached higher with his free hand and squeezed his fingers around the stone.

Now he was in motion, dancing slowly up the cliff. He kept the rhythm smooth, finding nubbins of stone for his fingers to cling to, and finger-width ledges where his foot could rest for a single breath. His eyes led the way. He felt the familiar emptiness of air beneath him and the exhilaration of it made him want to shout. The rock was warm and rough. Blood welled from a scraped knuckle. His muscles contracted, pulling him higher. He stopped briefly on the wider ledges, aware when he did of his bruises and scrapes. Soon he was in the shadow cast by the Beak. Where the cliff face met the sharper outcrop of the Beak, he found a large hollow in the stone. Aracco crouched there, resting, one hand anchored to the rock above him. He turned and looked across the cliff to find Valaren. His friend sat on the wide ledge of a mined vein, staring into the distance, his long legs dangling.

"Ho, Valaren," called Aracco, disappointed that his success had gone unnoticed. "Are you asleep?"

Valaren turned his head slowly. "Ho, Aracco," he called back, "did you fly?"

Cheered by the praise in Valaren's voice, Aracco stood up, balancing easily on the ledge. "See you on top!"

He turned and studied the pinnacle above him. From the ground, the rock had seemed featureless, but now he could see small cracks and ledges running toward the knife edge of the outcrop. He left the hollow and began inching across the cliff face. He still felt confident, but moved a little slower now. Sweat trickled down his back. A cool breeze tapped his shoulders. His knuckles stung. He reached out his hand for the next hold. Gray stone glittered here and there amid the dull yellow rock. For half a breath his thoughts strayed toward the eastern mountains. His right foot slipped.

His leg and arm swung over empty space. *Fool!* he

thought. His left hand strained to hold. His left foot swung him in. He slammed against the cliff.

His right hand raked across it, seeking hold. His fingers tightened and held his weight. He clung there, panting. A drumming sound, his heartbeat, pounded in his ears. His right foot scrabbled for another foothold. Finding it, Aracco cursed again.

Rockhead! Do you want to be ashes?

His legs were shaking. He forced himself to look at the rock, find the next hold, keep moving. His blood raced as he crossed the last few lengths to the edge of the Beak.

Aracco ascended the knife edge slowly, poised on fingers and toes. He was still shaking, but he kept his thoughts focused on the cliff. He jammed his hand into a crevice and felt it become firm, like a piece of the rock. Pulling himself higher, he found a new toehold and molded his foot to the stone. His fingers eased free of the crevice. His muscles flowed, sure and strong. Empty air was all around him, but he was of the rock again, solid, part of the cliff from one handhold to the next.

Swinging his foot up one more time, he wrapped his arms around the crowning pinnacle. His fingers curled along its stone. He tipped back his head and shouted. Echoing around him, he heard the pulse of rock and sky.

When his heartbeat slowed and he could feel his bruises aching, Aracco lowered himself into the depression on the shadowed side of the Beak. He scrambled up the short distance to the cliff top. On top of the cliff, along the edge of the ravine, gnarled trees grew, their trunks misshapen from the chafing of goldclimbers' ropes. Valaren was waiting for him there, lounging in the shade of a twisted old oak. His thin face shone with relief and pride.

"Well climbed!" he said. "Maybe you *should* be a climber. I'll wager you're the best route-finder the cliffs have seen since the days of Barak. It's the waste of a gift to make you a smith."

Aracco grinned at his friend's overflowing praise, then turned away, frowning down into the quarry. *What use is it to have a gift for climbing when everyone expects you to be a smith?*

Valaren unfolded his legs and stood up. "*Let's go see if your mother has a cure for aching stomachs. I'm famished.*"

They started along the upper edge of the ravine, following the cliff top until they reached the herders' road. As they turned onto the road, Valaren stopped suddenly. "Look," he said, "you can see the Great River!"

Following the direction of Valaren's gaze, Aracco saw the river valley through a gap in the foothills. Often it was veiled in haze, but today sunlight blazed clearly on the water. Like the eastern mountains, the Great River beckoned, flowing into the distance toward unexplored places. Aracco longed to follow it, to travel like the climbers did when autumn came, or better still, like one of the Osi, the wizardfolk. The

Osi went throughout Caraccen in their red-winged boats, bearing their wizardcraft. *What do they see,* he wondered, *on the far reaches of the River?* And how would it be to have that freedom, not bound by any guild, yet honored for one's craft? He gazed at the bright water, aching with the urge to know.

Valaren turned to face him. His cinnamon brown eyes were shining. "Is your father going trading?" he asked. "After we give gold to the River?"

Aracco nodded. "With my mother's people, in the desert." Several times a year, Aracco's father traveled as a trader for the goldsmiths' guild. In past years, Aracco had often gone with him, but this year, because of the mastersmith's contest, he would stay behind.

Valaren looked away again, toward the River. "I wish I could go with him. And I would like to travel further downriver—all the way to the sea. What is it like, I wonder?" His voice trailed off and he stared into the distance again.

Aracco gnawed his friend's words restlessly. It was unlikely either of them would ever journey to the sea. He knew Valaren hoped to become a trader, but even the smithy traders rarely traveled such a distance.

But I would go, he thought. *I would go, if I were free.* He felt closed in again, although he stood outside the smithy. His stomach grumbled and he nudged Valaren. "Hey, dreamer! Who was hungry?"

Valaren shook himself and leaped away. "Race

you!" he called over his shoulder. He sprinted down the road toward the village.

Aracco charged after him. It felt good to run, to leave his unsettled thoughts scattered in the road behind him. He felt his muscles stretching out. The sun shone in his face and the wind of running eddied past him. Squinting through the glare and dust, he tried to catch Valaren.

When they reached the village, the two boys ducked into the alley. Aracco pounded through the alley in Valaren's dust and swerved onto the road that led to the river. His father had built a house as a bride gift for his mother, just outside the village at the edge of the orchard. Before the whitewashed house stood his father's little smithy. As he raced past, he could hear the steady rhythm of a hammer. His father seldom came to the main smithy, choosing instead to work long hours at his own small forge. When he was younger, Aracco had helped his father almost every day. He had not questioned then whether he wanted to become a smith. He had been eager to be apprenticed and follow in his father's footsteps.

He caught up with Valaren outside the door of the house and stood gasping, out of breath. The scent of flowers drifted toward him from the orchard. Inside the house, he heard a girl's voice, familiar. Seri.

"Your sister's here," he said. "Helping my mother again. That means there will be food out!" Valaren bounded through the open door. Aracco followed.

Valaren's younger sister sat on a stool at the big oak table. At twelve years, Seri was small and strong, with rounded muscles in her arms. Her long autumn hair fell loose across her shoulders. From the wooden beams above her head, herbs hung drying. As they entered, she reached for the last of the seed cakes on the plate beside her. Aracco sprang forward and scooped up the cake from beneath her outstretched fingers. Leaping back, he saw that her brown hands were stained a dusty red. Seri whirled around, knocking over the stool, her hair swirling out around her like dark fire.

"That's mine!" she protested. He laughed and tossed the cake to Valaren. Her brother bit into it hungrily.

"Bless you, little sister," Valaren said between bites.

Seri stamped her foot and stuck her tongue out at Aracco. Then a mischievous smile lit her face. "There's plenty more," she said. "I'm helping your mother with the baking." She darted into the other room. Aracco heard her voice and his mother's answering.

Why are her hands red, then? he wondered. *They should be covered with flour.* Just then, Seri emerged from the cookery carrying a plateful of seed cakes. Aracco lunged for one.

"Thanks . . . Seri," he mumbled between mouthfuls.

Seri's smile still held a glint of mischief. "I made

the dough myself," she said. "Greedy one! Don't they feed you at the smithy?"

"We've been climbing," said Valaren. "Aracco climbed the Beak!"

Annoyance flashed across Seri's face. "Why do you climb," she demanded, "when you could be working in the smithy?"

Aracco choked on a piece of seed cake and bent over, coughing. *Who would want to stay in the smithy when he had leave to climb? I should want to,* he thought, feeling torn between two paths. It made him angry. He glared at Seri. "You wouldn't understand," he retorted.

When he saw her pained expression, he wished he had not spoken. As a child, Seri had played with the boys at being smiths. Now she, a girl, was barred from the guild. And she had loved their smithing games most of all.

She can have my place, he thought. *I don't want it.* But he knew well enough it was not his to give. And in the silence that held all three of them, he heard his father's hammer, ringing clear and steady, through the open door.

"Peace, you two," Valaren said gently, smiling at his sister. "You're right, Seri. We should be in the smithy, practicing for the mastersmith's contest."

Aracco groaned. In three weeks the four oldest apprentices would match their skills. The winner would earn the mark of first apprentice and gain much honor in the village. He knew all eyes would be upon him, his father's most of all.

"After the contest," teased Valaren, "when Aracco is first apprentice, he'll have no wish to climb."

"Speak for yourself!" retorted Aracco.

"He'd have no leave, more likely," Seri said, "working under the mastersmith's hand."

Aracco winced. If he won the contest, he would gain the right to serve Jeron, the mastersmith. Nago's father. He dreaded that fate even worse than the bellows. He would rather place second and gain the right to serve his father in the little smithy. But second place was no way to win his father's praise.

He realized that his father's hammer was now silent. His father appeared in the doorway.

"Seri, are those cakes ready yet?" Aracco's father asked. He paused, blinking, as his eyes adjusted to the dimmer light inside. Curran was a short, contented man. Like Aracco, he had tight-curled hair, but it was brown, not black. His skin was lighter too, a warm nut brown, like Seri's and Valaren's. He moved slowly, like a dreamer waking. When he saw the boys, a gentle smile spread across his face until it lit his eyes. His gaze rested longest on his son, in a searching, rueful way. "Home so early?" he inquired.

Aracco shifted, uncomfortable. His father's voice was mild, but in it he thought he could hear disappointment. And his careful gaze made Aracco feel like a flawed piece of goldwork.

Curran settled at the table beside Seri and cupped a seed cake in one hand. "Well?"

"They've been climbing!" accused Seri.

Curran stroked his pointed beard. "Shirking?" he asked, with a smile in his voice. "Or with leave?"

Aracco swallowed, seeking words. They came easily enough when he was with his friends, but he felt mute around his father.

"Curransmith," Valaren said, returning the smile, "with leave, of course."

"Aracco climbed the Beak," announced Seri. There was pride in her voice now, and she leaned against Curran's shoulder, gazing at Aracco.

"Did he now?" Curran smiled at her, then turned to face his son. His eyes still smiled, but his face was solemn. "Did you climb it well?"

Aracco looked back at him, his thoughts a jumble. How could he tell him how glorious it felt, in spite of almost falling, to climb the Beak?

"Like a master!" said Valaren.

Curran's eyebrows slanted up. "A master smith? Or a master climber? Whichever, I am glad it was well climbed." His brown eyes sparkled suddenly with mischief. "But perhaps I should scold you for climbing unroped?"

Aracco's gaze dropped to the table. He found his father's quick shifts of mood disconcerting. Curran's tone, half serious and half in jest, made him feel belittled. And his father's kindness only made it worse. *As if I'm but a child,* he thought, *not fifteen and soon to be a journeyman. I would rather be punished. If I felt I was his equal . . .*

"Back to your tasks at the smithy now," said

Curran, "both of you. And Seri . . ." Aracco's father gave her gleaming hair a tug. "Go and stoke the fire."

Seri darted toward the cookery, laughing. Aracco heard his father chuckle. Then Curran stood up, his eyes focused in the distant way Aracco's mother called his "smithing gaze." He went out the door, still holding the seed cake.

Aracco watched him go, feeling small. *But what, he wondered, can I ever do to feel myself my father's equal? I'll never be as good as he at crafting gold.*

A vision of the eastern mountains rose before him. *Find Terenger,* he thought. *Seek the streets of gold. That would gain me praise without staying in the blazed smithy. But I would need a wizard's skill to drive off eirocs. And the mastersmith would never grant me leave.*

3

The next day, Aracco was back in the smithy, polish-ing goldwork in the finishing room. He rubbed a drinking bowl with powdered clay, fidgeting on the bench. He hated sitting in one place all morning. This task was almost as bad as the bellows.

Across the room, Orin, the finishroom smith, stamped spots upon a golden leopard twice the size of his fist. The crouching leopard seemed almost ready to spring from Orin's melancholy hands. The powerful lines of the casting suggested that a living animal would soon emerge, tail and whiskers twitch-ing, from its bonds of gold.

My father's work, thought Aracco proudly. Al-though Curran, by his own choosing, did not hold the rank of mastersmith, he was readily acknowledged as the finest smith in Meged.

And his only son, Aracco brooded, *wants to be a climber.* He tossed a handful of clay into the drinking bowl, polishing it with the heel of his hand. *What would my father say if he knew? I wish I had the words to ask him.* His thoughts went around and around, rough as the clay.

"Aracco!" From the hallway, Gemmel's voice leaped to his rescue. "There are goldclimbers in the village circle."

Aracco set down the drinking bowl. Goldclimbers? In summer?

Last spring, when the climbers had passed through Meged on their way to the goldcliffs, Aracco listened eagerly to their stories. Muscular men and women, their hair and clothing dusty, they told of winter travels up and down the Great River. They had stayed in the village for a few days, then set off northeast toward the cliffs of Ramen. Ever since he heard their tales, Aracco had been restless.

He brushed the clay dust from his hands and glanced across at Orin. The dour-faced smith was absorbed in his craft. Aracco crept past him and out of the finishing room.

Gemmel stood waiting in the hallway, surrounded by piles of unsorted gold. The younger boy was as quick and graceful as a fish, with the sandy hair and blue eyes of his riverboat kin. He darted ahead of Aracco, toward the outer doorway of the smithy.

"Psst, careful," warned Gemmel, as he reached the door. "There's Jeronsmith!" They ducked into the

21

shadows of the doorway and peered out across the village circle.

Three goldclimbers stood beside Jeron, the mastersmith. One of the climbers was wounded. A red weal slashed his cheek and jaw. He wore the stunned look of a rabbit who has just escaped the talons of a hawk. *Had he fallen and somehow survived?* Aracco wondered. *And lost his nerve for climbing? Maybe. But why had* three *climbers left the cliffs so early in the year?*

He heard Jeron's voice, offering to guest them drinks at the inn. The mastersmith sounded grim. His tone sent a tremor of uneasiness along Aracco's spine. What was wrong? Climbers were always welcomed by the goldsmiths' guild. In spring and autumn, feasts were given in their honor.

In Caraccen, gold was common and valued far more in its crafted form than raw. The smiths of Meged forged gold into shapes of beauty to be used in ceremonies or worn to celebrate life. Their work bartered well and was held in high esteem all along the River. But without the goldclimbers, their forges would be silent.

"Why are they here?" whispered Gemmel, as Jeron herded the climbers toward the inn. "It's only midsummer."

Aracco shook his head, trying to dislodge his uneasiness.

"Maybe someone was killed," suggested Gemmel, "and they are taking his ashes to the River."

"Their hands are empty," Aracco said. "And why would they send three to carry one?" The climbers mounted the stairs of the inn and went inside. Jeron closed the door behind them. The silence in the village circle seemed ominous. Aracco felt as if a shadow crossed before the sun. Why was there no welcome for the climbers? "Come on," he said to Gemmel, "let's go back."

In the hallway, Gemmel returned to his task of sorting gold. Aracco went back to his bench. Puzzling over the climbers, he picked up the drinking bowl. He turned the bowl in his hands, looking for rough spots. *Maybe Gemmel is right,* he thought. *Maybe someone was killed. There is danger in climbing, that is certain.* He shuddered, thinking of his own near fall. *But that will not keep me from the quarry, any more than it would keep a climber from the cliffs. I would rather face danger than sit here in the smithy. If it wasn't for my father.*

If only I had a brother, he thought. *Then I would be free to choose another path. But, as it is, everyone expects Curran's only son to be a smith.* Until this year, he had not even questioned it. But now the smithy felt too small. His fingers tense, he plunged one hand into the powdered clay.

"Hey, Gemmel!" Nago's voice buzzed into the room from the hallway like an angry wasp. Aracco clenched his hand around the gritty clay. Nago was always looking for a fight. Often Aracco welcomed the chance, but not here, inside the smithy. He

23

glanced at Orin, hoping he had heard, but the smith was still intent upon the golden leopard.

"Did you see that climber?" Nago said to Gemmel. "The one who fell? Are you still fool enough to want to be a climber?"

"Shut your mouth, Nago." Gemmel's voice was urgent. Aracco knew why. When Gemmel's brother was killed in the quarry, his father had vowed none of his younger sons would be climbers. If his father heard Nago, Gemmel would land a thrashing.

Nago knows that well enough, thought Aracco, cursing the mastersmith's son beneath his breath.

"Who's to make me, Gemmel?" jeered Nago, even louder. "Not a scrawny would-be goldclimber!"

Aracco set the bowl down quietly and stalked to the door. As he stepped through the doorway, Nago looked up at him, his dark eyes narrowing. A smile flickered over his face.

"Gemmel," he snorted, "here's a desert warrior to defend you!"

Aracco gritted his teeth, fighting his desire to knock the smile off Nago's face. The punishment for brawling in the smithy would be harsh indeed. He might lose his place in the contest.

"Leave it, Nago," he snapped, "or I'll call Orin-smith."

Nago smiled again. "Are all Dahiri cowards?" Aracco's hands tightened into fists. Later, outside the smithy, Nago would regret this insult to Aracco's mother's people.

Nago took a step forward and kicked over Gemmel's carefully sorted buckets. Lumps of gold skittered on the stone floor; sungold, firegold, and moongold, gleaming as they mingled. Aracco growled, his anger rising. All Gemmel's work undone. And Nago would somehow duck the blame. It was so unjust! Suddenly he could see nothing but the hateful grin on Nago's face.

"River take you, Nago!" He lunged forward.

Smirking, Nago raised his fists. Aracco circled, waiting for a chance to smash him in the mouth.

"Nago." Valaren's calm voice spilled over them. "Your father wants you. He's in the casting room."

Aracco stopped, drawing in a long, slow breath. He remembered that he stood in the smithy and lowered his fists. Thank Barak for Valaren!

Nago's face soured. He turned on his heel and headed toward the courtyard.

"Close, Aracco," said Valaren, when Nago had gone.

"You're a liar, Valaren," retorted Aracco. "His father's at the inn."

Smiling, his friend scooped up a lump of sungold. "I'd forgotten," he said lightly. "But Dolansmith will keep him busy. Won't Nago be surprised!"

Aracco began to laugh. "I'd like to see him!" He imagined Nago sweeping up clay shards in the casting room with a face as long as a pica bird's tail. "He'll be wishing he had stayed at the bellows."

He picked up a lump of firegold and tossed it into

the bucket. Valaren stooped beside him, hunting out the pale moongold.

A morning's work scattered on the floor, thought Aracco. Inside him anger flared again. He longed to stuff his fist in Nago's mouth. *And if Valaren hadn't come along,* he thought, *I would have.* His hand closed around another piece of firegold.

"Are you going climbing?" Gemmel whispered to Valaren, his hands full of sungold. "This afternoon?"

Valaren shook his head. "We'll be working with Dolansmith again. We have castings to finish—gold to gift the River."

Tomorrow the whole village would travel down to the Great River to make their offerings of gold. Aracco and Valaren hoped to give their own offerings this year, if Dolan said their work was fine enough.

"I'm going climbing," Gemmel said, his face stubborn. "With leave or without it."

"Be careful, then," Valaren urged. "And don't be late for the feast."

Tonight there would be feasting in the guildhall to celebrate tomorrow's ceremony, and the unmarried women would dance for the gold. Aracco and Valaren had been casting gold for weeks in preparation, but Dolan, the casting room smith, had melted down all of their efforts, judging none of it worthy of the River. Today was their last chance.

But I'd rather go climbing with Gemmel, thought Aracco. He threw the last chunk of firegold into the bucket and went back to his bench, leaving Gemmel and Valaren to sort the remaining ore. Picking up the bowl again, he dipped his fingers in the powdered clay. *Gemmel's father,* he mused, *is set against him climbing, but he goes anyway. I would never shame my father so. Still, I wish there was some way I could leave the smithy.*

At midafternoon, Aracco headed toward the casting room. Last time he and Valaren had worked with Dolan, they had carved wax in the shape of their castings, and coated the wax with clay and cinders. Today they would pour gold to replace the wax, and see the mettle of their work.

Valaren caught up with him halfway across the courtyard.

"Whew!" he exclaimed, "I thought I would melt if I stayed at that fire much longer."

"Out of one fire and into another," replied Aracco. "Working with Dolansmith will be just as hot!" They tiptoed into the casting room. Dolan stood at the hearth, pumping the bellows. In the coals, gold-filled crucibles were planted.

Dolan raised his shaggy head and scowled. "Now we'll see how good your crafting is," he said fiercely.

Aracco braced himself, but inside he was smiling. Dolan was as unpredictable as an old badger. Aracco liked him. You never knew what he would say from one day to the next, but he always spoke his mind. Unlike Curran, whose silences made Aracco wonder what his father found lacking.

The smith nodded curtly toward the ledge where Aracco and Valaren had left their balls of clay. "Let's begin!"

Valaren carried his clay mold toward the hearth. "If it is well cast," he said solemnly, "this gold will gift the River."

Dolan chuckled. "And if it is not? You'll be begging gold from Aracco, then. The full moon rises tomorrow."

Tomorrow they would watch the dancers throw golden offerings into the River's muddy current. Not raw gold, but forged gold, the best that the guild at Meged could offer, for the River was life. Without it, the land of Caraccen would be as barren as the desert where the Dahiri roamed.

Valaren poured liquid gold into the spout at the top of his clay mold, then stepped back, his face flushed with heat. He lowered the mold into the cooling trough. Aracco heard a loud crack as the clay ball split open. Water hissed and bubbled around the gold inside. When the water quieted, Valaren pulled out his mold and settled at a bench to remove the clay pieces that still concealed his crafting.

Aracco walked over to the ledge. He stood for a moment, looking at his ball of hardened clay. Hidden within the rough sphere was the graceful shape of a bird. Today he would watch his crafting burst full-fledged from its clay egg. He carried his mold to the fire, feeling as unsettled as the flames. Why make birds of gold at all? They would never fly, never equal the beauty of real birds.

Under Dolan's fierce gaze, he raised a crucible in the tongs and watched liquid gold flow into the clay. Gold bubbled suddenly to the surface of the spout. He set down the crucible. Water spurted around his mold as he quenched the gold in the cooling trough. Gold gleamed through cracks in the clay. When it had cooled, he sat down at the crafting bench and began working loose the cracked clay. Like bits of shell, the clay shards fell to the bench. On the pile of rubble a golden swallow rested, its wings and forked tail open to catch the wind. For a moment, he felt himself soaring like a bird. Then a shadow fell across his casting and Dolan's huge hand closed around it.

Dolan turned Aracco's casting in his hands. Aracco watched him, fearing that the smith would crush the bird's fragile wings with his words. He knew he could not bear to see it melted down and lose its only chance to fly.

"Well enough," said Dolan grudgingly. "You have your father's eye for the form. Even if you lack his patience."

Aracco relaxed a little as Dolan's hand released the bird. *Dolansmith,* he thought, *has a tongue like a bee.* Even his rare words of honey held a sting. Still, the old smith had compared him to his father. That was praise indeed. Could he someday become his father's equal as a smith? It seemed impossible. But he would have an offering to give the River.

Aracco tensed again, watching Dolan examine Valaren's casting. It was perfect; every angle of the running antelope was true. He could almost see the wind along its dappled back. *It's far better than mine,* thought Aracco with mixed relief and shame. What fault can the old grumbler possibly find? A faint smile touched Dolan's mouth, then was gone so quickly that Aracco doubted he had really seen it. Dolan set down the golden antelope.

"Worthy of the River, Valaren."

Aracco tossed a clay shard into the air and caught it before the smith could notice. Worthy of the River! From Dolansmith that was praise indeed! Surely Valaren would win the contest. Aracco secretly hoped his friend would earn the mark of first apprentice. Valaren would not mind working with the mastersmith. *And if I rank second,* thought Aracco, *I'll be assigned to work with my father.* Maybe then it would be easier to tell him of his longing for adventure.

"Off with you both to the finishing room," growled Dolan. "Else you'll be late for the feast."

In early evening, Aracco and Valaren crossed the alley to the guildhall, their finished goldwork in hand. Inside the hall, countless lanterns illuminated the painted walls and polished floor. At intervals, upright wooden planks were set into the mud-brick walls. On winter feast days the boards were removed and fires built inside the openings to heat the hall.

Long tables ringed the dancing circle. At the mastersmith's table across the hall sat Aracco's father.

Curran was laughing, his dark brows slanting up with joy. He turned to whisper something to Aracco's mother. She sat beside him, carrying the mark of her desert blood in her dark skin and black cloud of hair. As always, she wore it proudly. *But then she is a full-blooded daughter of the desert,* thought Aracco, *not half-caste like me.*

He had started toward them, wanting to hear his father praise the golden swallow. But now, halfway across the hall, he hesitated, afraid his father would show disappointment. His mother was leaning toward Curran, smiling like a girl in love. Their delight in each other was a shining circle, but he no longer felt he stood inside it. His unspoken desire to leave the smithy set him apart. He turned away, glancing back over his shoulder. His father's golden cup was raised, honoring his mother.

Aracco sat down beside Valaren at a table near a planked section of the wall. Feeling glum, he set the golden swallow by his plate.

The younger apprentices came clustering around them. Taz hovered at Valaren's shoulder like a loyal herder's dog.

"Have you heard?" Taz said. "Jeronsmith has decided to add casting to the tasks."

"But you can't make a cast piece in a day," said Valaren.

"You can pour it," Taz said. "Jeronsmith says that is where the skill shows. All the flaws are seen when the hot gold flows."

Taz had a habit of talking in rhyme. *He'd make a good rhymer,* thought Aracco. *He remembers every tale told in the village circle.* "That's five tasks in the contest then," said Hod, counting them out on his fingers. "Casting, sheetwork, engraving, finishwork, and melding." Hod reminded Aracco of a tortoise, solemn and slow-moving.

Aracco counted faces: Taz, Hod, and Emen. As usual, Gemmel's younger brother, Emen, was dreaming on his feet; staring across the hall, his blue eyes unfocused.

"Where's Gemmel?" asked Aracco. Emen blinked and gazed around at them. He looked bewildered, then concerned.

"Don't worry," said Valaren reassuringly. "He'll show." Sure enough, just as the mastersmith took his place at the head table, Gemmel slipped in beside his brother.

"Where were you?" whispered Emen.

"Climbing," said Gemmel, resting one hand, closed in a fist, on the table. Emen glanced nervously at their father, three tables away, but Gemmel was too excited to give him heed. "Look!" he said, opening his hand. Gold gleamed on his palm. The nugget was the size of an apricot pit and yellow as the eyes of a goat.

"Sungold," breathed Taz. "The sorting smith will give you praise for this find!"

"One might think you were apprenticed to the cliffs," said Valaren.

Gemmel was suddenly still, which was startling in someone always in motion. "I'm going to be a gold-climber," he said quietly. "You'll see."

There was a hiss of breath from the other boys, and Emen shivered like a rabbit. Aracco felt a stab of envy. Gemmel seemed so sure, and almost eager to defy his father.

"I don't see why you want to be a climber," said Hod. "Mostly you'd be hauling baskets of gold down the cliffs."

"Like hauling charcoal for the fires!" added Taz.

Gemmel turned the nugget between his fingers. "They can't always get to the gold from above," he said. "Someone has to find the new routes and set toplines."

"That's dangerous work," Valaren said softly. Everyone was silent, remembering the death of Gemmel's older brother. And each autumn when the climbers returned with their baskets of gold, they brought stories of those who had fallen.

"Worth it," said Gemmel. "You've seen the nuggets they find! As big as my fist, dozens of them."

"But you're a goldsmith's son," protested Hod. Aracco felt as if the words were meant for him. The men of his own father's line had been goldsmiths since the first guildhall was founded in the city of Baraken. He had always known he would continue that tradition. But Gemmel's words made that path seem bitter. He chewed them slowly throughout the meal, grinding them between his teeth.

33

Across the room, the mastersmith stood and raised his golden cup. "To the River!" he said. Dozens of voices took up the cry. When the noise subsided, Jeron spoke again.

"May the smiths of Meged always prosper. May we walk with honor in the footsteps of our elders, father to son, and craft our finest work to gift the River. Let us celebrate the Caracmeren, for the River is life." He nodded to his eldest daughter. "Ophira, will you dance?"

As Jeron's daughter glided to the center of the hall, Aracco heard the master's words still ringing in his ears. Father to son. In the footsteps of our elders.

He looked across the hall at his father. Their eyes met and Curran smiled, his eyebrows slanting. Aracco returned the smile, but his shoulders hunched as he felt the unseen bonds tightening around him. What else could he be but a smith?

*M*usic gathered around Ophira. *The melody pulsed*
with the rhythms of Meged, the ring of hammers
passed from hand to hand through generations. This
dance too was part of tradition, giving gold to the
dancers so that they might gift the River.

The mastersmith's daughter wore a shimmering
green dress. Bracelets sang on her slender wrists and
ankles, and her straight black hair flowed down to
her hips. The air around her seemed to crackle. She
curved one arm toward the musicians with extrava-
gant grace and began to dance.

Aracco watched, resentful, unwilling to be moved.
He did not like Ophira. In her own way she was as
bad as Nago, teasing the journeymen until they stam-
mered. To escape from watching her, he looked
around the hall. The men's faces made him squirm.

35

They stared at Ophira like desert squirrels fascinated by the lure dance of a snake. He glanced at Valaren—and froze.

Gazing at Ophira, Valaren wore a distant look, as if his eyes were fixed on some far horizon. He often wore that expression when he spoke of adventure, but now he wore it for a woman. Aracco's heart grew tight inside his chest. He felt invisible and voiceless. If he leaped up and began to shout, he doubted Valaren would notice. Bewildered, he turned back toward Ophira. What was it about her that made his friend a stranger?

Ophira's face was dreaming in the dance; dark lashes brushing acorn brown skin. *She moves like one of the Dahiri,* he thought, *as wild as night on the desert.* He thrust the thought away, angry to find himself thinking of Ophira with favor. She whirled and swayed, drawing his gaze with her. Ophira's dancing held him motionless, until, with a final grace that tied a knot in his stomach, she sank to the floor and waited with her arms outstretched. Across the dancing circle, Hod's brother Chak sprang to his feet, his blue eyes shining.

"Ophira! Take this offering!" Chak threw his crafting toward her and it tumbled through the air, gleaming bright. Ophira raised her proud head and caught the goldwork in her skirt. More golden offerings took wing and she spun around to catch them, her face soft with pleasure. Aracco heard the offerings clink against each other, the sound as rapid as his heartbeat. Then a voice across the room called Seri's name, and another voice took up the cry.

"Dance, Seri! Dance!"

Ophira stepped back, her cheeks flushing as if she had been stung. Aracco had seen her look that way before, at the gathering fire, when another dancer drew the crowd's attention from her. Ophira's face was very still; he thought of the air that comes before a storm. She walked slowly toward the edge of the dance circle, her back straight and taut.

"Ah, Ophira," Aracco heard Valaren murmur. "There are eyes still watching you. And I would give you honor." His friend scooped up the golden antelope. "Ophira, catch!" She turned, caught it in her skirt, and stood smiling at Valaren.

Aracco sat trapped inside the glow. He glared at the mastersmith's daughter, not understanding his friend. How could Valaren choose *her* to give his crafting to the River? A casting Dolan had praised! Half angry and half fascinated by her beauty, Aracco stared at her until Ophira turned away.

He watched, still scowling, as Seri darted to the center of the hall. Valaren's sister was really too young to dance for the gifts. She was not yet a woman, had not passed her first blood, but she was well loved in the village and honored thus for her skill as a dancer.

Seri stamped one foot and raised both arms in a joyful silent shout. The music danced beside her as she wove summer through her footsteps. Her movements flowed like the River. She leaped, landing poised to jump again like a young green frog. The watching crowd began to stamp its feet and clap. Aracco felt his hands uncurl.

"Dance, Seri!"

Her tangled hair bounced on her shoulders and her brown arms praised the music. Aracco tapped his foot and smiled. He watched her bounding like a young herdbeast in the spring. She kicked up her heels, dodging an unseen shadow, then chased a wisp of melody around the circle. The music curled into her arms and out through her footsteps. Seri spun around, arms held wide, and came to rest as the music faded. Aracco sighed without knowing it, and jumped to his feet.

"Seri!" She faced him, radiant, and made a basket of her skirt. The golden bird flew from Aracco's hand into its bright nest. A shower of offerings followed the bird, so many that she could not catch them all. The clear song of gold jingled and chimed on the polished floor. Seri leaned down to gather up the offerings. Laughing, she carried her skirtful of gold from the dancing circle and came to sit beside Valaren.

"Well danced, little sister," said Valaren proudly.

Seri dimpled, then glanced at Aracco.

"I thought," he paused, trying to describe the joy in her dancing, "you were just like the herdbeasts in spring."

Seri's dimples vanished and she stuck out her

tongue. "In that case," she retorted, "I'll not give your crafting to the River. I'll melt it down instead!"

Aracco stared at her. How could she even suggest such a thing! Seri? Reforge his bird? "What do you mean, *you'll* melt it?" he demanded.

"What do you know of forging gold?"

Seri clapped her hand over her mouth. Her brown eyes grew wide as those of a startled deer.

"Oh," she said quickly, "I didn't mean . . . I mean I'll ask Valaren. *He'll* melt it for me!"

"Peace, Seri," said Valaren. "If a Dahiri likens you to a herdbeast, you should feel honored!"

Aracco bristled. "Watch your tongue, Valaren." He needed no reminders of his mixed blood. Nago had taunted him about it until the word "Dahiri" tasted bitter in his mouth. If he were truly one of the Dahiri, he would be riding free across the desert, not stifling here inside the guildhall.

Valaren spread both hands palms up. "Peace, I say again. I meant no insult. No more arguments, I ask you. Tomorrow we give gold to the River."

In the gray light of dawn, the procession formed in the village circle. The dancers gathered behind the mastersmith, carrying the offerings in baskets. There were five dancers this year, including Seri, who bounced from foot to foot beside the mastersmith, chattering at him like a pica bird. Jeron smiled down at her, the usual stern expression gone from his face.

Aracco turned his back on them, disconcerted. He

could never understand what words Seri found to share with the mastersmith. One might almost think they were friends. Shifting his heavy pack on his shoulders, he followed his mother and father down the line of villagers. Kalisha and Curran walked arm in arm, she in a simple white dress, he in the brown traveling tunic of the guild. After today's ceremony, Curran would set off on his trading journey to the desert. This year neither Aracco nor his mother would go with him. "I am needed here," she had said. No one questioned a healer's mindsight, so his father would travel downriver alone.

"Barter well for us, Curran," a woman called to his father as they passed. Her white dress gleamed with gold thread sewn in water patterns.

"Don't give a goldweight more than you must to those heathen Dahiri," advised an old man. He brandished a wine flask.

Aracco bristled and moved to stand beside his mother. Her dark brown skin looked almost black against her white dress. Any fool could see her kinship with the desert tribes.

"Hush," urged the old man's wife, nudging him hard with her food basket. "Mind the healer." The man's mouth dropped open and he bowed to Aracco's mother.

"No insult meant, Kalisha," he said.

"And none taken, Hagan," replied Aracco's mother, "but try to speak less about that which you know little."

Aracco glanced sideways at his mother. Her face showed no sign of the anger he knew she must feel. *Hagan's a fool!* he thought. *No insult meant? Does he think it no insult to mock the Dahiri before a daughter of the tribes?* He wanted to shout it in the old man's face but knew his words would be unwelcome. Instead, he walked stiffly by his mother's shoulder, wondering if she ever regretted leaving the desert.

"Aracco!" Valaren waved as they approached. Like Aracco, he carried a pack full of the trade gold that Curran would take downriver.

The village beekeeper called to Aracco's mother. "Kalisha, can you look at my son's arm? He burnt it on the wax."

Aracco and his father fell into line beside Valaren while his mother went in search of the beekeeper's son. Aracco watched her go. She moved with long, easy strides, carrying her healer's kit and an empty basket for gathering herbs along the riverway. As she passed, the villagers bowed slightly. Kalisha was honored by most in Meged for her wisdom and her skill as a healer.

The procession began to move in a straggling line through the village and across the bridge that spanned the Meged River. There the road curved, following the little river on its journey toward the Great River, the Caracmeren.

Aracco walked beside his father and Valaren, envying the easy companionship between them. Valaren did not hesitate in telling Curran of his dreams.

41

"I want to travel," Valaren was saying, "and not just on the easy routes of trading. Is that not strange?"

"Very," teased Aracco's father. "Perhaps you are one of Osiann's children, and not your father's son at all."

Doubting it, Aracco glanced up the line at Valaren's father. He had the same lanky frame, the same red-brown hair as did his son.

"With my long nose?" exclaimed Valaren. "You are jesting!"

"True," replied Curran, "but listen to my story. It is told in the desert." Valaren's eyes brightened and Aracco moved closer to listen.

"The Dahiri tell a tale," said Curran, "of the Lord of Desire. He is the one we call Osiann the Elder, father of wizards.

"One night every year, the Lord of Desire chooses a woman. He comes to her in the moonlight, his hair a silver halo around his ageless face. She is blessed by his touch and honored with his child.

"When Osiann is gone, she remembers, but has no words to speak of it. And her heart holds both joy and sorrow. For when the child is grown, it will leave her."

Curran paused and Aracco felt his gaze, smiling but a little sad. *Why sad,* he wondered, *when I'm bound to be a smith?*

"When her child is grown," his father continued, "it will feel the call and travel downriver, past the gates of Kune, until it comes to the wizards' city. And there be taught the wisdom of the Osi. That urge to seek the wizards' city is the same strong desire that I feel for working gold, and you for traveling."

"But can the urge to travel be called a gift?" asked Valaren. "Perhaps I have no gift at all."

Curran laughed. "You have a gifted tongue!" Then his face grew serious and his eyes rested once more on Aracco. "Sometimes one's gift comes where least expected. It is so far away or so near at hand that we do not see it clearly."

"You speak in riddles, Curransmith," Valaren said.

"Like a wizard," Curran replied with a grin.

A seriplover skidded past, and Aracco's father turned to whistle at the bird.

But has everyone a gift? Aracco wondered, echoing Valaren's words. *Perhaps I have no gift at all.* His father's story explained nothing, and the talk of wizards made him feel more unsettled than before. He wished there was no contest, so that he might go downriver.

As the sun rose higher, it grew hot on the road through the grassy hills. Flasks were passed along the line, and voices murmured, speaking of the ceremony and the feast that would follow. Beside Aracco, Valaren brushed back his tangled hair. He passed a water flask to Aracco's father.

"I'll be glad to be rid of this pack," Valaren said. "The journey home will be lighter."

Curran poured water over his head and, like a wet

dog, shook the drops at Valaren. "For some," he replied. "If the trading goes well, my pack will be even heavier." He smiled as he said it, looking more like a jester than the finest smith in Meged. In his pack, he carried smithing tools for mending any goldwork the Dahiri might have broken. On his return journey, he would have not only the tools, but cured skins, dates, and a flock of herdbeasts to tend.

"You will have the herdbeasts to carry your burdens," said Aracco.

Valaren laughed. "You must be of the Dahiri indeed, Aracco, if you find traveling with herdbeasts easier than carrying the load yourself."

Aracco scowled and kicked at the dust. When there were herdbeasts in the village, Nago's taunts always doubled. *He'll have fresh dung for insults when my father returns,* he thought.

Valaren spread his hands, palms up. "I meant no insult, Aracco. Only fools scorn the Dahiri: desert riders, masters of the wind."

"And only a greater fool," added Aracco's father, with an amiable nod up the line at Hagan, "would mock their women. Consider Mahala."

Aracco grinned. Despite his mixed feelings about his Dahiri blood, he was proud to be kin to Mahala, his mother's sister. She was the leader of her Dahiri camp. Mahala was no taller than his mother, but as solid as a rock in the shifting desert sands. Nago's insults would slide off her without impression. He glanced at his father, grateful for the image. But now

44

Curran was gazing down the line at Kalisha, a quiet smile rounding his face. Aracco felt closed out again.

When the sun stood overhead, they came out of the grassy hills and saw the Caracmeren. A huge brown river, it filled the plain and stretched endless into the hazy distance. Aracco took a breath and let it out slowly. Every year he was awed by the River.

It is so big! he thought. And then, more reverently, added silent words of greeting. *Lifebringer! We come to give you honor.*

The River gave life to Caraccen. On both sides of the Caracmeren, the plain sprouted green. The Great River watered the olive groves that cloaked the lower slopes of the Barren Mountains. Its broad back carried the riverboats, linking the guilds and the people of Caraccen. And every spring the floods came, renewing the fields.

Below him, a long causeway sloped up across the wide flat beach to meet the wharf. In autumn, when the goldclimbers came down from the cliffs, the wharf would be crowded, but now a single hand's count of boats were moored beside it. Tomorrow his father would take passage on one of those boats and travel downriver to trade with the Dahiri. Aracco listened to the creaking spars and the cries of birds flying over the River, wishing with all his heart he was going too.

Turning away from the causeway, Jeron led the procession along the beach to a low stone point jutting out into the River. The gray stone beneath

Aracco's feet was worn smooth by spring floods and passing generations of goldsmiths. As he watched the mastersmith walk to the offering rock at the tip of the point, Aracco could hear the deep voice of the River. Below the rock, the River turned in the endless swirl of a whirlpool.

Jeron raised his arms and began to speak. In his hand, a golden cup flashed in the sunlight. Crafted by Aracco's father, it would be the First Gift. "We give praise to the River . . . the River is life . . . take these gifts with honor . . ."

As the familiar words rolled over him, Aracco added his own silent prayer. *Oh, River, let me prove worthy of my father's praise.*

"Be it so," said Jeron. He released the golden cup, hurling it skyward in a shining arc. The villagers echoed his words.

"Be it so," Aracco spoke the blessing with them, watching the First Gift descend toward the unseen whirlpool. He hoped that it carried his prayer, but over the voice of the River, he could hear the birds calling, "Downriver . . . downriver . . ."

Jeron spoke again. "Oh, River," he said, "your waters flow from the cliffs of the mountains. You know of the goldcliffs. From the wealth of these cliffs we craft the gifts we offer in your honor. We ask your blessing, Great River. May gold flow from the cliffs with the abundance of your waters."

Something in his tone made Aracco shiver. He remembered the three climbers standing in the village circle. Why *had* they been in Meged? Other than a few whispers between apprentices that day, nothing had been said about their presence. So perhaps it had been no strange thing after all, only the death of a climber.

The mastersmith stepped back from the point and bowed his head. Aracco and the others did the same. In the hush that followed, he heard Ophira's bracelets sing as she walked to the offering rock. Without meaning to, he raised his head, and then could not look away. He watched as one by one, she gave to the River the smiths' offerings she had gathered in the dance. Her white skirt fluttered in the river wind, outlining the curve of her hip and thigh. Aracco stared, heat rising through his body. His face was even hotter with shame. This was no way to honor the River! His gold was not in her basket, and he had no right to watch her gift the River. He wrenched his gaze away and stared at the stone beneath his feet.

He heard Ophira's bracelets sing again as she curtsied to the River and withdrew to the edge of the circle. Aracco raised his head again. Seri was next. She had gathered his gift, and custom gave him right to watch *her* offerings.

Seri's bare feet were silent on the stone. Gold flashed through the air as she made her offerings. He saw his golden swallow rise in her hands, then plummet toward the water. Gold followed gold until the basket was empty. Seri set down her basket on the stone and raised her arms into the wind like a

47

dancer. She stood poised above the whirlpool, honoring the River. Aracco's heart beat faster.

"Take my gift, River," he whispered, "from the hands of your dancer. May it ride your current to the desert of my mother's people. Let that which is forged in fire, seed of the sun, be the vessel holding my desire. Wash me clean of wishes that I may not own. And let me gain my father's praise."

Seri lowered her arms and picked up the basket. As she left the point, she curtsied to Jeron. He raised his head and bowed gravely, as if she were the lady of a guildhouse in Baraken. The next girl stepped forward with her basket of gold, and Seri slipped back to the circle.

Aracco lowered his head, not feeling cleansed at all. There was a heaviness inside his chest. He heard the River flowing past him, toward places he would never travel. The mastersmith would not choose him to be a trader. He had no skill with words. What use were his dreams of adventure? He was a smith's apprentice and would someday be a smith. Trying to hold the intent of his prayer, he clenched his fists until his knuckles turned pale brown. But images formed in the stone beneath his feet; the pinnacles of mountain cliffs no one had ever climbed. With an effort, he again turned his thoughts to the River and listened to the splashes of falling gold.

When the last of the dancers had given offerings, the mastersmith stepped forward again. "Great River," he said joyfully. "Now we feast in your honor!"

Cheers rose into the wind. The villagers began to sing, trooping in disorder toward the beach. A feast was spread out on the sand and everyone gathered around it. Aracco's father raised a cup of wine.

"I give toast to the River!" he said. "May it flow forever!"

"To the River!" Cups were raised, emptied thirstily, and filled again. Aracco settled on the sand. He tore a large chunk from a loaf of bread and passed it to Valaren, saying, "For this bread, we thank the River."

When they had eaten their fill, Aracco and Valaren crossed the beach. At the far end, bluffs rose out of the River. The rocks were solid, with plenty of holds. They clambered up and over the top of the bluffs to explore the rock face above the water.

Although the cliffs were of no great height, Aracco's pulse quickened as he climbed, hearing the River move below. When he reached the top again, he settled on one of the flat wide rocks. Looking down across the beach, he could see the villagers still feasting and hear their laughter. It was only a short drop to the sand, but he had no wish to join the crowd. While he waited for Valaren, Aracco turned to face the River.

Hala birds skimmed above the water, red wings flickering. Boats passed, riding down the brown back of the River or moving laboriously upstream against the current. Around the boats flashed the halas, always curious. Valaren hoisted himself over the edge of rock and sat down at his side.

"This is far better than sweating in the smithy," said Aracco.

Valaren frowned. He had been strangely quiet, Aracco realized, ever since they reached the River.

"What is it?" Aracco asked.

"If not for the contest," said Valaren, "I would ask leave to go downriver with your father."

"Downriver . . .," called the hala birds. "Downriver, downriver . . ."

Aracco stared at the slow brown current of the River. If it were not for the contest, he thought, *I too would ask leave.* The River was a pathway to the desert, to the camps of his mother's people. The Dahiri roamed free, following their herds, unconfined by walls of stone. As did the riverboat crews. Envious, he watched them ply the River.

Long oars dipped into the current, and dun-colored sails flapped as they were trimmed. Like delta geese, the riverboats flocked upon the Caracmeren, their captains calling out to one another as they passed. Among the others, he saw a small boat moving swiftly upriver, its red sail round with wind. At the helm a man stood alone, clad in a sky-blue robe.

"Look, Valaren!" Aracco said. "There's one of the Osi!"

The boat's red sail was as bright as the hala birds that hovered all around it, dipping their wings in greeting. Other boats slowed as the wizard passed, their crews and captains staring.

"I wonder where he is going," mused Valaren.

Aracco watched until the red sail disappeared in the distance, envying the wizard's freedom. The Osi came and went as they pleased, answering to no master. When he was a small boy, one of the Osi had passed through Meged. The wizardwoman had come to visit his mother. She had wrinkled, weathered hands, he remembered, but her face was as smooth as a girl's. He had perched on a stool, listening to their strange talk of healing, drawn to it but understanding very little.

"He comes from the City of Wizards," Valaren murmured. "What is it like, I wonder?"

Aracco blinked, rousing from his memories of the healing wizard. "My father says none of us will know," he replied. "He says only the Osi travel the River Kunar, and they do not speak of their city."

Downriver of Baraken, the River Kunar split off from the Caracmeren, carving a narrow canyon through a spur of the eastern mountains. Some said Osiann the Elder himself had created the river, seeking a swift path to the eastern sea. Only the wizards had magic enough to pass the gates of Kune and return upriver against the rough current of the River Kunar.

Or is it craft? wondered Aracco. The wizardwoman

had not spoken of magic, only knowledge and herbs. He frowned, trying to remember, but Valaren's voice called him out of his thoughts.

"Look! There's a boat from the delta."

The deltaboat drifted past, moving downstream. It seemed stout and snubnosed beside the riverboats. The other boats gave it a wide berth, scattering like ducks before a caiman. The awnings hanging over its deck were the same dull green as a caiman's scales. The long poles lashed along its sides served as oars upon the delta.

"Has your father been there?" asked Valaren.

"Once," replied Aracco, watching the deltaboat with longing. "Years ago, when he was a journeyman. He says the River splits into a dozen channels on the delta, weaving through the marshes on its way to the sea."

"I would like to see the delta," said Valaren, his brown eyes shining. "And I would like to travel on the sea."

I would like to journey even to the desert, thought Aracco, *and ride across the sands with my cousin, Segev.* He thought of the desert sands stretching out from the Dahiri camp, as endless as the sea. Despite the prayer he had spoken to the River, he felt as restless as ever. *If I had been born of the desert . . .*

His thought was cut short by the squeal of an animal in pain. Aracco scrambled across the top of the bluff and jumped, landing on the sand below. He straightened up and hurried toward the sound, with

Valaren close behind him. Ducking around an outcrop of stone, he halted, bristling.

A small gray rock hare cowered, trapped against a rounded hollow in the bluff. Nago loomed over the hare, jabbing at its hind leg with a long, sharp stick. Blood stained the sand and the point of the stick. Aracco rushed forward, grabbed the branch and felt it snap under his hands. He flung the end aside and spat insults at Nago.

"Coward! Pig slime! Legless lizard!" Nago whirled to face him, brandishing the stick.

The rock hare squealed again. Aracco crouched beside it and touched the animal's dense fur. He felt its small heart fluttering.

"Hush, little one," he said. "I'll not harm you. Hush." He began to whisper to it, words his mother had taught him in the Dahiri tongue. His fingers found the wound. It seemed shallow, but still . . .

"Herder!" scoffed Nago, leering down at him. "Dung hands." Goldsmiths were of higher worth, his tone implied, than those who followed the herds. Aracco glared up at Nago.

Valaren stepped forward. He raised his hands and placed one foot between Nago and Aracco. "Leave it be, Nago."

The mastersmith's son sneered and thrust the end of the broken branch toward Valaren's chest. Valaren stood motionless, while the rock hare shivered beneath Aracco's hand. Its fear sent a chill racing up Aracco's spine. He crouched frozen, staring up at Valaren and Nago. The jagged end of the stick hovered a fingerwidth from his friend's body. The air smelled of blood. Suddenly, Nago flung down the branch and stalked away.

The tension went out of Valaren's shoulders. "Let's go find your mother," he said. His voice was shaking.

Aracco picked up the hare, cradling it in his arms. "Thank you, Valaren," he said softly.

"That pitiable swine," said Valaren. "Next time . . ."

"Next time I'll kill him!" Aracco vowed.

Valaren gave him a pleading look. The rock hare shuddered. "Let him be, Aracco. Just stay out of his way. He's not worth a week at the bellows."

"He's pig slime," said Aracco, "and I'll get him!" As they approached the feasting villagers, he could see Nago farther down the beach, trading jests with a journeyman.

As if nothing had happened, he thought, tightening his hold on the rock hare. It squeaked in protest. "Forgive me, little one," Aracco whispered, and turned his back on Nago.

His mother sat at the edge of the crowd. "Kalisha!" called Valaren as they drew near. "We have need of a healer."

"What has happened?" asked Aracco's mother. She took the rock hare from his arms. Aracco could feel the animal's trust in her as he let it go. All hurt creatures seemed to sense her skill. Once she had even healed an injured wolf.

Valaren put a warning hand out to quiet Aracco. "It was Nago," he said. "With a stick."

Kalisha glanced across the beach at the mastersmith's son.

"Poor child," she murmured. "He feels so much pain." She opened her healer's case. Aracco stared at her in disbelief. How could she spare sympathy for Nago? True, his mother was dead, and his father wore a face like stone, but that was no reason to torment a rock hare. He sensed that his mother was aware of his unspoken questions, but she made no reply. Quickly she fashioned a poultice and laid it on the wound, all the while speaking softly to the hare in the Dahiri tongue. A pool of silence grew around them as those nearby stopped eating or talking to watch. She held the poultice in place with one hand and stroked the hare's ruff with the other.

"This little one will heal quickly," Kalisha said. She removed the poultice from its leg and coated the wound with a pale green paste. The rock hare had stopped shivering. It nibbled eagerly at a grape leaf that Valaren held. Aracco watched the hare until he realized that his mother was watching him. Her dark eyes flashed a challenge.

"But what of you, my son?" she asked. He fidgeted beneath her gaze, feeling her healer's touch upon the knots inside him. It hurt, and he ducked away from her eyes, staring at the sand.

"I thought as much," she said. "You had best go trading with your father. I will speak of it to the mastersmith."

Aracco stiffened. Here was the leave he wanted! But his father's trading journey might take as long as a week, and the contest was less than three weeks away. Could he afford to lose so much crafting time? The rock hare sat up on its hind legs and took another grape leaf from Valaren's hand. Watching it eat, he wondered what to do. He could follow his heart and go downriver, or strive to become worthy of his father's praise. He remembered the prayer he had offered to the River. If it was to be granted, he should try his best to be a smith.

"I will stay," he said. As he spoke, he felt a heaviness settle in his chest. The day seemed oppressively hot. He thought of the bellows with loathing.

His mother's eyes flickered. With pride or disappointment? When she spoke her voice was even, and he could not tell.

"You must choose your own path, my son."

As if, he thought glumly, *I truly have a choice.*

Valaren looked troubled. Aracco searched his friend's face, uncertain. *Did I choose rightly? Is it better to gain the crafting time and risk a fight with Nago? If I find him tormenting another creature, I will . . .*

"Might I go?" asked Valaren suddenly. He leaned toward Aracco's mother. The greens in his fingers fell to the sand, and the rock hare moved forward to nibble them.

Kalisha smiled at him. "Curran's load will be light with you in his company."

"But, Valaren," protested Aracco, horrified to

think his friend might go without him, "what about the crafting . . . ?" Seeing the excitement on Valaren's face, he bit off the words. Even with one week less to practice, Valaren still had skill enough to win the contest. *How can I ask him to stay?* A hard lump of pride was forming in his throat and his own choice tasted bitter. He wanted to say something, change his mind and go, but his pride was choking him, making it impossible to speak at all. The rock hare finished the last of the greens and scurried off across the sand. Aracco swallowed hard, closed his mouth, and said nothing.

Forlorn, Aracco tagged along when his father approached one of the riverboat captains, a tall, serious woman, and began bargaining for passage downriver. Aracco sat beside Valaren on the wharf, listening to them haggle over pieces of goldwork. The captain turned one piece, a gleaming bracelet, over and over in her calloused hands.

"Is this your work, Curran, smith of Meged?" she asked.

"No, one of the apprentices crafted it." Rousing a little from his misery, Aracco stared at the bracelet. A rising phoenix formed the band, its wings and tail flowing through the gold. The work was cruder than his own, but he could feel its power.

"It is rough work," said the captain.

"But it shows great promise," replied Curran firmly. "One day the name of this apprentice will be known in every guildhall."

Aracco was puzzled. He had never seen the bracelet before. Which apprentice could have fashioned it? And to whom did his father offer such praise? He felt a surge of jealousy, wishing his father would say as much of him.

After a few more rounds of bargaining, the captain held out her hands, palms up, accepting the bracelet and a smaller piece in trade. Aracco carried his father's pack of trade gold onto the boat and placed it under the central awning. He felt the boat's gentle tug against its moorings. Misery settled on him like a sullen cloud.

When evening came, the villagers gathered their empty flasks and baskets, standing on the beach in small, cheerful clusters. "Trade well for us, Curran," they said. "Good journeying."

"Good journeying," Aracco echoed, but could not meet Valaren's eyes. He watched his father and Valaren walking up the causeway toward the river inn. The villagers were starting home along the road to Meged. Aracco lagged behind, gazing back up the causeway. Then, shouldering his mother's basket of herbs, he slowly turned away.

The following days were dull without Valaren. With her brother gone, Seri did not come to work in his mother's house. When he asked his mother why, she smiled and would not say. The house lacked warmth without his father's presence, and the smithy was intolerably the same. Haul water, polish gold, tend the fire, carry fuel. He wanted to go climbing, but with determination turned his back on it and used the time for crafting gold. Working in the constant clamor of the smithy, he tried not to think about the quarry or the desert or all the other places he would rather be.

When he arrived at the smithy on the sixth morning, he found Gemmel standing by the slate where apprentice tasks were posted. Looking up at the slate, he saw a bucket drawn beneath the cloud leopard that was the sign of his father's line.

"Waterboy," said Aracco. "It could be worse. What's your lot, Gemmel?"

"Bellows." They both groaned, then Aracco burst out laughing. Gemmel's long face reminded him of a disgruntled herdbeast.

"Trade you tasks," offered Gemmel.

Aracco shook his head, still laughing. "Not for all the gold in Terenger," he said. "But maybe you can wriggle out of it. See you at noon." He picked up two buckets and headed toward the well. Hauling water was dull, but far better than the bellows.

The smithy was built around a large courtyard. The hard-packed earth would be glaring hot by afternoon, but now the white clay still held last night's coolness. In the center of the courtyard, a low stone wall rimmed the well. Aracco lowered the first of the buckets until he heard it splash and felt it sinking slowly. He hauled it up, hand over hand. The line was rougher than a climbing rope, but it filled his mind with images of the quarry. Suddenly, he felt intolerably restless. This afternoon, when he was given leave, he would go climbing. He filled the second bucket and started cautiously toward the first of the cooling troughs. If he spilled any of the water, he might well find himself at the bellows. Water was honored in Caraccen and never wasted.

There were five hearths in the smithy. Each had a cooling trough beside it where the hot gold could be plunged. Every night the troughs were emptied into channels that led to the orchard, and every morning they were refilled with clean water. Aracco filled the stone trough beside the central forging fire, refilled the buckets, and started toward the fire in the jewelers' quarter.

The corridor was noisy with swallows. Their mud nests decorated the beams overhead. Among the nests overflowing with young birds were the cracked remains of other nests. When the birds had first laid their eggs in the spring, he had discovered Nago knocking nests off the beams with a long pole. Eggs fell and shattered on the packed earth while the adult birds circled.

That fight with Nago had almost landed them both in the well. But it had been worth every bruise. Aracco grinned. Nago had caught full blame that time, not from the mastersmith, but from Dolan. The old smith's love for birds equaled his passion for cast gold.

Aracco emptied the buckets into the cooling trough in the jewelers' quarter, letting his footsteps match the light rhythm of their hammers. As he returned to the courtyard, Taz darted past him.

"Valaren's back!" Taz called over his shoulder.

Aracco dropped the buckets by the well and sprinted toward the village circle. His friend stood near the inn, surrounded by herdbeasts. As Aracco approached, Valaren pushed his way through the herd.

"Aracco! There is so much to say. You should have come."

6

Even those few words were enough to fill Aracco's mind with visions of the desert. He gritted his teeth to keep from groaning. He'd been a fool to stay behind! He glanced over at his father, who stood outside the inn, talking to the mastersmith. Despite having stayed in Meged, Aracco felt no closer to accepting the path of a smith. And his father seemed as distant as if he stood upon the far bank of the River.

"Segev asked after you," continued Valaren, "and Aracco, there's a girl . . ." Just then, the younger apprentices came crowding around them with questions.

"How was your journey?" Gemmel asked.

"What did you see?" demanded Taz. "Tell us. Quickly!"

Valaren spread his hands, as storytellers do when

they are ready to begin. The apprentices fell silent. Valaren's clear voice drew images from the journey.

"We reached Baraken at midmorning on the second day. The River was crowded there, with more boats than I have ever seen in one place flocking to the city."

Aracco's thoughts wandered, remembering the city from his own journeys to the desert. The city of Baraken was built upon a hill. Mud houses crowded the river bank and lower slopes, and above them were the sandstone houses of the guilds. At the crest of the hill stood the House of Barak.

Hero, the people of Caraccen had named him. Barak b'Osiann had been one of the Osi. He had brought crafts up the River Kunar and founded the guilds. All of Caraccen heeded the wisdom of Barak's teachings and followed the laws of the Council, save the Dahiri tribes. And because the people of the desert lived apart, they were scorned by many in Caraccen. But Aracco knew the Dahiri were wise and proud and free. Men like Hagan were fools! With a shake of his head, he brought his attention back to focus on Valaren's tale.

"When we reached the desert," his friend was saying, "Zamir, the Dahiri trader, met us with horses. The desert horses run so smoothly you think they are standing still, but the wind goes rushing past your ears. And in the Dahiri camp, I met a girl. Her name is Shifra. . . ." Valaren paused and sat there, staring at nothing. Watching him, Aracco felt a sound inside his head like the howl of a jackal. He shivered and moved a little closer to his friend. What was happening to Valaren?

"Go on," urged Taz. "What of Shifra?"

Valaren spoke again, but he sounded far away. "She is small and quiet and her face is like the moon. All the Dahiri men are in love with her. I did not really understand until I saw her dance. When Shifra dances, she moves like fire."

Listening, Aracco wished with all his heart he had gone to the desert. He had not, and now he felt his friend moving away from him into unknown places.

Nago emerged from the smithy. The mastersmith's son strolled closer and every angle of his face was hatefully familiar.

"And what of the trading?" asked Hod, as Nago joined them.

"Zamir is clever," replied Valaren, "but not as quick with words as Curransmith. Look at all the trade goods and the herdbeasts he gained for two sacks of gold."

"You smell of herdbeasts," Nago said, his voice low and biting. "Do all of the Dahiri stink?"

A hot wind rose up inside Aracco. He sprang forward, raising his fists. He wanted to strike out at something, and as usual, Nago was asking for a fight.

"Aracco!" Valaren warned. He nodded toward the mastersmith. Aracco lowered his hands slowly, keeping them clenched. "The Dahiri," Valaren said to Nago, "speak with gracious tongues, even when they are in pain." Glowering, Nago turned away.

Scorpion, Aracco thought. He wanted to rub Nago's nose in the dirt and wipe the pride from his face. He wanted to pounce, but as an apprentice, he was bound to follow the laws of the guild. Barak's laws. Since the days when Barak b'Osiann had founded the guilds, feuding had been unthinkable. Only the Dahiri still fought among themselves, raiding one another's camps.

I wish I was in the desert, he thought. *There I could answer Nago's insults when they were given.*

Instead he glared at his enemy's back as the mastersmith's son retreated across the village circle. A crowd was gathering as people emerged from the smithy and surrounding houses. Among them, Valaren's sister stood out like a poppy in the summer fields.

"Look!" exclaimed Valaren. "Seri is wearing red." The color signified a girl's first blood and passage into womanhood. Seri's dress was blood red and fringed with tassels. Aracco stood frozen, watching the tassels brush her brown legs as she ran to greet her brother.

"Valaren!" Seri flung her arms around her brother. She emerged from his hug and looked around at the other apprentices. They were silent, gazing at the girl in the blood red dress. Emen's face flushed a deeper brown when she looked at him, and Aracco felt a reflection of that heat on his own face. He fought it with a grimace. Seri turned toward him, her smile uncertain.

"Aracco?" she said, her voice suddenly shy. He stared at her, dumbfounded. She took a few steps backward.

"So, little sister," said Valaren, his face proud. "You are a woman now."

Seri ducked her head, then dimpled at her brother. "Tomorrow is the seventh day from my first blood."

"Tomorrow then," Valaren said, "you will be clothed in gold. I am glad we returned to see you honored."

Aracco said nothing. He could not stop staring at Seri. Had she really become a woman? The idea would not fit comfortably in his mind. It jostled inside his head until the pulse in his temples began to throb. If Seri was a woman . . . His eyes followed the graceful line of her neck down to the brown hollow of her throat. He swallowed, choked, and began to cough. Seri looked at him, her brown eyes soft with concern. She stepped forward again, extending her hand.

"I'm all right," he gasped, terrified that she might touch him.

Seri lowered her hand and stopped, looking hurt. "Aracco," she said, "what is wrong?"

He struggled to reply. "Nothing," he sputtered. "Nothing's wrong." He knew as he spoke that the words were a lie. Suddenly, everyone around him was changing. Valaren was in love with a girl of the desert. And Seri, Valaren's little sister, was a woman.

On the following day, everyone left the smithy at noon. Aracco changed into festival clothes at home.

Then he and his father walked together toward the house of Seri's mother. Kalisha had gone there in the early morning to help prepare Seri for her rites.

Curran was silent as they walked. His eyes were distant and his face content, lost in daydreams. Aracco kept pace with his father, his own thoughts churning. He wanted to ask him to explain—why is everyone so different suddenly? And why am I the same? But he feared the answers, and the habit of not disturbing his father was very strong. He had learned as a small boy not to interrupt his father at his work. And never to ask questions when Curran wore his "smithing gaze."

Outside the house of Seri's mother, they found places among the men who lined the street to the river. Inside, he heard women's voices. There was a sudden chorus of laughter, followed by silence. Then his mother's voice rose above the others, leading the women in a chant as they readied Seri for her rites of passage. The words were unclear, muffled by the walls of the house. But the power of the women's chant flowed over him and made a hushed and breathless pattern in the air. His hands began to sweat.

At last the door of the house opened. Seri's mother emerged, holding one ribbon of the passage veil. Aracco's mother stepped out behind her, holding another. Beneath the veil Seri stood hidden. Aracco caught one glimpse of her gold-dusted feet before the rest of the women streamed out of the house and surrounded her completely. They held the white veil suspended from red ribbons, shielding her from view.

As the women moved along the street, gold pieces sewn to the edge of the veil began to chime. The men followed in an uneven procession. At the riverbank they spread out along the rocks overlooking three deep pools. The pool in the center glistened; beneath still water the sand shone gold. Aracco stared hard at the river, his breath fast and shallow. A breeze crossed the surface and he shivered. The women's voices rose in a song he had heard only twice before, the hymn of a young girl's passage.

The last words soared over the water. On the final note, the women swept back the veil. Clothed only in gold dust, Seri stood poised on the rocks at the river's edge. She dazzled his eyes, shining from forehead to toe like a golden phoenix. Gold flecks shimmered in her hair. A sigh swept the riverbank like wind, and the water trembled. Aracco drew in his breath. She was a woman of gold, cast by a mastersmith, every line perfect.

Seri raised her arms and dived into the pool. Startled by the splash, his heart began to pound. The river gleamed with falling gold. Seri disappeared among the shining ripples. Moments later, she emerged, her red hair sleek and water-dark. She scrambled out of the water, naked, her wet skin gleaming with oil and flecks of gold. Aracco felt liquid fire leap inside him. He squirmed, trying to escape, but the heat was rising, searing through him. He could not look away. He stood trembling and breathless, his gaze sliding down the wet curves of her body.

Dark hands drew a cloak over Seri's shoulders—his mother's hands. The heat inside him drained away. He stumbled in the wake of the procession, shaken and hungry. At the head of the crowd he heard Seri laughing. The sound was so familiar that his shoulders straightened and his footsteps grew more certain.

In the guildhall, tables were laden with food. Aracco slid onto a bench and stuffed a chunk of bread into his mouth. He chewed and swallowed, feeling less shaky. As he ate, he watched Seri move among the tables, clad now in a new white dress, and smiling at the villagers who raised their cups in her honor. She was light-footed, cheerful, and entirely familiar. Aracco grinned and tore off another piece of bread. In some ways, at least, she was still the same. Voices called out as Seri passed, teasing her.

"Which man among us will you choose, Seri?" called one of the journeymen. Aracco choked on his mouthful and his face grew hot.

"Keep your silence, Seri," counseled Kalisha. "Let them wonder."

"The journeymen will be casting courting gifts soon," called Aracco's father. He raised his cup to Seri with his slow, gentle smile.

"And the apprentices will be casting looks alone."

Taz's older brother grimaced with mock pity. "Poor lads! Can't choose a woman until you're a journeyman."

Aracco saw Emen's face darken. Aracco tore at his chunk of bread, wishing he dared hurl it at Taz's brother.

"Seri has time enough." From across the hall, Jeron's cool voice washed over him. "And she has more to choose than a man." A brief silence settled over the table, as the apprentices and journeymen pondered the mastersmith's words.

"What does he mean?" whispered Gemmel.

"Maybe Osiann is her father," suggested Taz.

Valaren laughed. "Don't be foolish, Taz. Do you see a wizard's mark about her?"

Aracco's eyes followed Seri. Her red hair was still flecked with gold, but despite the honor given her this evening, her face showed no sign of self-importance.

She's the same, he thought, feeling reassured. Valaren's sister treated admiration like sunshine—turning toward its warmth but never clutching at it. Maybe she was a woman now, but she was still Seri.

"Dance, Seri!" shouted someone. A chorus of voices echoed the words.

"Dance! Dance for us, Seri!" She walked to the center of the room and motioned for the music.

As she began to move, Aracco felt his throat tighten. Her dance was joyful, as it had been the night before she gave gold to the River, but there was a difference. It was hard to see her as Valaren's little sister when she danced that way. Heat rose through his body. He felt tied to her—on strings—tugged by her every movement. Her hair swept down her back and billowed like flame. He wanted to touch that fire. His breath became uneven, watching her swirl and leap. The lamplight shimmered on her nut brown skin, and her body found a rhythm to caress the music. He wanted to be there, caught within the circle of her movement. The tassels of her dress hovered around her legs and arms; like a cloud of butterflies they folded their white wings as the music faded.

"Seri!" called Valaren, raising his cup. "I give you honor!"

Smiling, Seri curtsied to her brother. She came to sit beside Aracco, her face flushed and bright with pleasure. The fragrance of scented oil spilled over him. Feeling dizzy, he shifted on the bench, putting a safe distance between himself and Seri.

"Aracco," said Valaren, "what of you? Will you not toast my sister?"

He raised his cup awkwardly, and some of the wine washed over the edge, flowing cool across his fingers. He stared down at the dark red drops pooling on the table. Seri was a woman now. He didn't know what to say.

"You dance," he said, "like one of the Dahiri." He knew his words were flat and lame as soon as he had spoken. They did not echo with the power and wild beauty of the desert. Farther down the table, Nago laughed. Seri flinched and her shoulder touched Aracco's.

"Some honor," scoffed Nago. "You might as well wish her to bed with a herdbeast."

Aracco sprang to his feet. Faces turned all along the table, glaring at Nago. Dolan slammed down his fist, rattling the plates.

"Watch your tongue!" shouted the old smith. Across the room, Jeron raised his head and surveyed the uproar coldly. Nago stared at his plate, avoiding the accusing glares. Aracco felt satisfaction cool his rage. For once, the scorpion had stung himself as well. A girl's passage rite was a time of respect and honor for her womanhood, not of crude words. Even Nago, who had gained apprenticeship bereft of his mother's teachings, knew that.

He'll be at the bellows tomorrow, Aracco thought, *if I know anything of Dolan!* He glanced cautiously at Seri. All of the light had gone out of her face. He wished he had the skill with words to coax it back again. He wanted to touch the gold in her hair and tell her that she moved like fire.

"Aracco does you honor," said Valaren softly. "You would know this if you had seen Shifra dance."

Some of the brightness returned to Seri's face. Aracco looked at his friend, grateful, envying Valaren's ease with words. He set down his cup. It clanged against his plate.

"Shh," said Gemmel. "Listen." Outside, Aracco

73

heard the sound of a rope slapping the wooden planking. "Goldclimbers!" Gemmel and Aracco traded glances. Again? They were all listening now, intent upon the sounds. Everyone watched the guild-hall door.

"What are they doing here?" asked Valaren. "They never come down from the cliffs in midsummer."

But three climbers had, Aracco thought, *just past a week ago. Why had so little been said of it then?*

"Maybe they've found a new lode!" said Taz.

"Maybe a cliff's gone fallow." Emen's words brought a silence. When a vein had been quarried an arm's length deep, it was abandoned. Any deeper and the work became too dangerous. In the days before Barak had formed the guilds, whole cliffs had collapsed, hurling climbers to their deaths.

One by one, seven goldclimbers filed into the hall. Two of them were women, with black hair pulled back into long dusty braids. The climbers' faces were burned almost as dark as Kalisha's by the sun, and their leggings and loose shirts shimmered with gold dust. A buzz of conversation rose to greet them, filling the hall. No one wanted to be rude and ask the obvious question, but Aracco heard it whispered all around him.

"Why are they here?"

" 'Tis the wrong season. Why are they here?"

"Trouble, I'll wager."

"Why are they in Meged before autumn?"

Jeron stood up, bowing to the climbers. "Welcome

to Meged," he said. But his tone bore little sign of welcome. His stern voice reached across the hall, stilling the questions. The mastersmith beckoned, inviting the goldclimbers to join him at the head table. Aracco's father stood, offering his chair to one of the climbers. When they had settled, Jeron raised his golden cup. "To our guests," he said. "May your days of climbing be long and filled with gold." Dozens of drinking vessels, gleaming in the lamplight, were raised in reply.

One of the climbers rose to his feet and spread his hands palms down, shaking his head. "Thank you for your gracious words," he said, "but we cannot drink this toast. We are leaving the cliffs." His tone was somber and heavy with loss.

7

An anxious silence fell over the hall. Gleaming cups were lowered slowly, hitting the tables with muffled clinks. Aracco shivered, chilled by the tone of the goldclimber's words.

"Leaving the *goldcliffs*?" Hod whispered. His shock was reflected on faces all around the guildhall. The mastersmith set down his cup.

"What is the cause?" Jeron asked slowly, as if he did not want to know or feared to give offense. Guild matters were a guild's concern. It was rude to question a climber about such things. Still, the doings of the goldclimbers were of great importance to the smiths of Meged.

"It is the death hawks," replied the climber, a tall, thin-faced man. "The dirty eirocs. They have come to Ramen." Startled gasps whispered through the hall.

Aracco leaned forward, his heart thumping. Eirocs? He had never seen one, but the herders spoke of them and avoided the highest pastures where the death hawks hunted. Herdbeasts that strayed too high were seldom seen again. But eirocs never left the mountains.

"They were sighted almost two weeks ago," said the thin-faced man. "Several climbers fled after the first attack."

Aracco shuddered, remembering the wounded climber and his companions who had passed through Meged. Had Jeron commanded silence?

"Since then the eirocs have come every day to plague us."

"Two climbers carried off yesterday," said a second man, a stocky climber with a reddish beard. He slammed his fist on the table, clattering the dishes. Horrified whispers echoed his words, hissing through the air like open wings.

"Carried off?"

"Climbers?"

"And one the day before that," added another climber. Her low voice rippled with sorrow.

Aracco felt stunned. He felt as if the guildhall was crumbling around him. Such a thing, death hawks on the goldcliffs, was unheard of. Beside him Seri shivered, her face pale. Valaren's eyes were wide, staring at the climbers. Across the hall, Aracco saw his father bow his head. And his mother's face reflected the woman climber's grief.

"I'm headed toward Baraken," declared the red-bearded climber. "There's work in the city."

"But the eirocs!" said Valaren's father. "They've never been seen on the goldcliffs. In the mountains, yes, but never so low."

"Maybe they have eaten all the goats," said the thin-faced climber. "Whatever the reason, we are leaving. The earnings from goldclimbing are not enough to risk being bird's meat."

"Can't you drive them off?" demanded Dolan. The red-bearded climber sprang up, knocking his chair to the floor. Jeron spoke quickly. Aracco could not catch the words, but the mastersmith's tone spoke a cool apology for Dolan's rudeness. The climber sat down again in the chair Jeron offered, glaring at Dolan.

"We have tried," said the thin-faced climber wearily, "and set watchers on the cliffs, but it does no good."

"And the guildmaster paces the quarry, helpless and half mad with sorrow," said the low-voiced woman.

"Others will be leaving soon enough," added the second woman. "There's talk of it at all of the fires. The cliffs are a risk a climber takes willingly, but these eirocs . . ."

Murmurs of shock and consternation rumbled through the guildhall, growing louder and louder.

"What of the gold?" muttered Dolan.

"What will we craft if the climbers leave the cliffs?"

"Where will we get our gold?"

"There's darkgold," suggested a journeyman, "from Gamelon upriver."

"It's difficult to work," Hod's father countered, "good only for cups and flagons."

"What of Terenger?" asked Taz, his voice piping above the uproar.

"Yes," agreed an old smith, nodding his approval at Taz. "What of the golden streets of Terenger?"

Suddenly, tales of Terenger flowed through the hall. In his mind, Aracco saw again the gray heights of the eastern mountains. Beyond them lay the streets of gold. If the goldcliffs were threatened, would some seek Terenger? He glanced at Valaren and saw his friend's eyes shining with excitement.

"It's only a story," said Hod's father. "And even if the streets *are* paved with gold, no one who seeks Terenger ever returns."

"Eaten by eirocs," muttered Dolan.

Jeron raised his arm, and the seal ring on his hand flashed. "Enough," he said firmly. "Let us remember that we have guests. And tonight we honor Seri's rites of passage. Let this matter rest. The guildhall council will meet on it tomorrow."

In the morning, while Aracco stood before the task slate in the smithy hallway, Emen came up beside him.

"Gemmel's gone," said Emen.

"What do you mean, gone?" asked Aracco, turning

to stare. Emen stood straight and taut, no longer settled comfortably in daydreams. Suddenly he looked a lot like his brother.

"He's run away," replied Emen, his voice quavering.

To the goldcliffs, thought Aracco. *Gemmel has run off to join the climbers' guild.* He felt a surge of envy, despite the news of eirocs. Seeing the worry creased in Emen's forehead, he tried to reassure him. "Gemmel's quick," he said. "He'll land on his feet."

Emen's face relaxed a little, looking hopeful. "Do you really think so?" he asked, his tone still anxious.

Aracco nodded, but he was anything but certain. Gemmel was clever, but was he quick enough to evade a swooping eiroc? And would the climbers welcome a boy who had broken bond with his guild? Apprentice vows were not taken lightly.

Maybe now they will, he thought, *now that the eirocs have come.*

He watched Emen scurry toward the casting room, then started toward the charcoal storeroom. It would feel good to be rid of these tasks. He could not take Gemmel's path and run away, but if there were a way to be free of his vows without shaming his father . . . He thought of Terenger and the eastern mountains. If there were an honorable way to seek them, he would go.

He opened the wooden door of the storeroom and went inside. The room was cool and dim; the only light came in through the open door. Black dust rose as he began to fill the buckets. Outside, a shadow darted past. The door swung shut. Through the heavy wooden door, Aracco heard familiar laughter. Nago!

He flung himself against the door. Too late. Nago had dropped the crossbar into place. He was locked inside.

Aracco paced the little room, fuming. Wait until he caught hold of Nago! His foot met one of the buckets and he stumbled. Looking down, he could not see the bucket or the floor. Darkness surrounded him, black as charcoal. And he could not get out.

Panic rose in his throat. Fighting it back, he reached down, fumbling, until his hand closed on the bucket. He threw it at the door. The noise was deafening. And satisfying. He groped around, found the other bucket, and hurled it after the first. *Clang!*

Aracco stumbled over to the door. He beat upon it with both buckets, wishing it was Nago's head. *Clang, clang, clang, clang!*

Suddenly the door swung open. He looked out at Hod's astonished face. Aracco lowered the buckets slowly, blinking in the sunlight. "Thanks, Hod." While Hod stood at the door, still staring, Aracco scooped charcoal into the battered buckets.

Raging inwardly at Nago, Aracco paced from one forge fuel bin to the next. He became aware of the fearful voices of those around him, and his anger died away.

"What is Meged without gold?"

"If all the climbers leave the cliffs . . ."

"Where will we get our gold?"

Hammers paused, then struck again with anxious vigor. The news of Gemmel's disappearance soon spread through the smithy, further upsetting the rhythm of work. The gold seemed to jangle as hammers struck and the air hummed with tension. First the eirocs, and now this. Never before had a Meged apprentice deserted his guild. And so renowned was the smithy that only a handful of its apprentices chose other paths once their apprenticeships were served.

Aracco was in the forging room when he heard the thump of hurried footsteps. Gemmel's father stormed through the room. The apprentices cowered at their benches. Whispers followed him like windswept leaves.

"He's been talking with Jeronsmith," ventured Taz.

"Will they send searchers after Gemmel?" asked Hod.

"He's still an apprentice," said Hod's brother Chak. "He owes his time to the guild."

Rad, the forging smith, set down his hammer and turned toward the apprentices. "If he's gone to the goldcliffs," the smith said firmly, "there will be no search. The mastersmith's not fool enough to start a quarrel with the climbers' guild. Not anytime and certainly not now."

The whispers settled into silence. They all knew where Gemmel had gone. Rad's hammer rang out again and, one by one, they returned to their tasks.

Aracco returned to the storeroom for more charcoal. Carrying the heavy buckets, he started toward the casting room. As he stepped through the archway into the room, he heard Nago's voice jeering. "Your brother's gone to the cliffs. Too bad, Emen. He'll be eaten by eirocs for certain!"

Emen crouched at the bellows, staring up at Nago like a frightened hare. Aracco tightened his grip on the buckets, fighting the desire to heave them at the back of Nago's head. *Where, by the River, is Dolan?* he thought. *Everything is so askew. If I start a fight in the smithy today, the mastersmith will likely bar me from the contest. I can't risk that. I'll settle my score with Nago soon enough.* Aracco clenched his teeth, thinking hard. *What would Valaren do if he stood in my place?*

Stall Nago, he thought, *until Dolansmith returns.* Loosening his hold, he let the buckets clatter to the floor. Nago's head jerked around, his mouth open. Slowly, he backed away, slipping out of the room through the far archway. Aracco stood there, sur- rounded by the scattered charcoal, too astonished to move. Then he heard footsteps and felt a strong hand grip his shoulder. Turning, he faced the mastersmith.

"Finish your task and go," said Jeron, his eyes as hard as stone. "Emen, I would speak with you."

Aracco gathered up the charcoal hurriedly and fled outside, glad that he had held his temper. He had never seen the mastersmith look quite so cold.

When all of the fuel bins were full, Aracco took his

place beside Valaren in the forging room. Slowly, they pounded ingots into sheets of gold. More than once he saw the forging smith pause in his work and stare off at nothing, letting his hammer dangle. At midday, the mastersmith sent Taz around with a summons calling the smiths and journeymen to the guildhall.

Rad set down his hammer and blinked at the apprentices. "You may as well be off," he said. "There'll be no more work today." Aracco and Valaren exchanged glances.

"The quarry," breathed Aracco. "Let's get out of here!"

"Taz," called Valaren. The younger boy spun around, pausing in the courtyard archway. "Tell the others. We're going climbing!" Aracco wanted to cheer. Valaren's words were like a strong breeze sweeping through the gloomy smithy.

Aracco stopped at Chak's bench on his way to the door. Hod's older brother was raising the sides of a cup, stretching the gold with even strokes of his hammer. "Come on, Chak," he said, "we're going climbing!"

Chak looked up with a scowl. "Go away," he growled. "Can't you see I'm working?" He stared down again at the cup in his hands, his dark brows drawn together. Stung by Chak's rudeness, Aracco hesitated. Then Valaren's voice touched him lightly.

"Let him be, Aracco. Ever since the contest was announced, he's been acting like a journeyman."

Aracco turned and headed toward the door again. What a fool Chak was! Choosing to sit inside when they had leave to climb. As he followed Valaren outside, he heard the steady clang of Chak's hammer, the only sound remaining in the empty smithy.

The younger boys crowded around Aracco and Valaren as they started up the road, asking nervous questions about Gemmel and the council. Nago was there too, walking a little apart from the others. Aracco glared at him, but Nago didn't seemed to notice. The mastersmith's son, his face sullen, carried some of the gloom that had filled the smithy. His presence cast a shadow on the afternoon.

"What of the gold?" asked Hod. "What will they decide to do?"

"And what if the eirocs come here?" asked Taz. Everyone halted, glancing nervously up at the sky.

"Don't worry," said Valaren. "They won't come this far from the mountains."

"And they've plenty of climbers to feed on," muttered Nago.

Valaren swung around before Aracco could even raise his fists. "Shut your mouth!" he said. "Shut it, or go back to the smithy."

The apprentices were startled. Valaren never lost his temper. Nago looked stunned. His mouth snapped shut and he moved away from the others. *Maybe he'll turn back,* Aracco thought hopefully, but when he glanced over his shoulder, Nago was still following the others up the herders' road.

When they reached the quarry, Aracco took the ropes and climbing gear out of the cave they used as a cache. He put on a climbing belt and attached a climbing iron to the front of the belt. The interlocking rings of the climbing iron made it easy to control the flow of the rope, whether one was tending line for a climber, or cliff-walking down from the top of a climb. Not that he intended to use a rope. But the younger apprentices would, and later on he would be tending line.

"Taz," he said, "you and Emen set up the toplines." His fingers were itching to touch the rock, but he waited while they scrambled up the path and looped the ropes around several of the old oaks that served as anchors. Then Taz and Emen descended on two of the lines, walking slowly down the cliff. When they reached the ground, Hod and Emen paired up on one line. Taz and Valaren took the other. Nago strolled away from all of them to climb alone. Seeing everyone in place, Aracco moved swiftly to the cliff and curled his hand around the stone.

Once he started to climb, Aracco forgot about the goldclimbers and Gemmel and everything but the rock beneath his fingers. He followed a narrow crack up the unquarried face beside the Beak, fitting his fists between the stone and shaping his feet to the holds. He felt like a waterglider; the stone was a river and he rode its current toward the sky.

After a while, the crack widened out and formed a quiet ledge. Aracco floated onto its surface and sat down, becoming himself again. His knuckles stung and there was a cramp in his left foot. Kneading it with one hand, he looked around to find the others. Hod was tending line for Emen; Taz belayed Valaren on a route up the quarried stone; and Nago . . . Aracco frowned. Nago was climbing the Beak.

Rockhead! thought Aracco. *He hasn't the skill for it. Not without a topline.* He watched Nago's slow progress up the cliff. A few moves forward, pause, a little flourish, another move, flourish.

Like a rooster, thought Aracco, *showing off.* Nago reached the bird's eye hollow and started across the cliff face toward the knife edge. Aracco drew in his breath as Nago reached for the sharp edge of rock. *Too soon!* he thought. Nago's left foot slipped. Loose stones went bouncing down the cliff and clattered on the floor of the ravine. Swiftly, Nago pulled himself to the edge of the Beak and clung to the stone like a baby on its mother's breast. Across the empty space between them, Aracco could see him shaking.

Give it up, Nago, he thought. *Call for help and I'll set another topline.* But Nago was silent. *Fool,* thought Aracco. *A good climber knows when he's beaten.* He could tell that the mastersmith's son was too scared to move.

Serves him right, he thought, remembering Nago's laughter as he slammed the storeroom door. *I'd like to leave him there a few days.* The image of Nago clinging to the cliff until he was humble enough to beg for help was so pleasant that Aracco savored it.

He would finish his climb in a minute or two and throw down a topline. The mastersmith's son was in no danger, unless he moved.

And he won't, thought Aracco. *He's stone frozen!* Nago looked as though he was melded to the cliff. His hands and feet seemed part of the rock.

Good, thought Aracco, *no chance of him peeling off before I set the line.* He stood up, turning to face the cliff, and reached for his next hold.

"Hang on, Nago!" Valaren's voice echoed in the quarry. Aracco looked down. His friend had unclipped from his line and was moving sideways on the cliff below Aracco, crossing from the quarried rock to harder routes. Aracco tensed, watching him. It was very like Valaren to go to Nago's rescue, but why climb the Beak unroped to do it?

Hey, Valaren! he wanted to yell, do you think you can carry him down? But he feared to break Valaren's concentration with a shout. He found each hold before his friend reached it, silently urging him on. There was a queasy feeling in his stomach. Valaren did not have the skill. Not to climb the Beak unroped.

At least he isn't showing off, Aracco told himself. Valaren's climbing held no flourishes. Watching his friend move steadily across the cliff, Aracco began to relax. Maybe he'd been wrong. Valaren was a better climber than he'd realized.

But why doesn't he just set a topline? What does he think to do when he gets there? Uneasy questions churned inside him. He held his breath, watching Valaren ascend the cliff until all three of them were at the same height, separated only by the endless air between them. When his friend reached the hollow below the Beak, he breathed out again, relieved.

"Stay there, Valaren!" he shouted, but Valaren called out to Nago at the same moment and did not hear him.

Aracco watched Valaren move onto the ridged stone that led to the knife edge. He was still climbing smoothly, but a little too slowly. "Almost there," Valaren called to Nago.

Don't stop, Aracco pleaded silently. *Keep going! A few more moves and you've got it.* The tension began to leave his arms. Valaren was almost there. He saw his friend reach for another hold, fumble, and peel off the cliff like a falling stone.

Aracco's vision blurred and he closed his eyes. He clutched the stone he faced in desperation. The ledge beneath his feet seemed to be moving.

Earthshake! he thought. *The cliff's going!* Heart pounding, he waited for the rocks to split around him.

After an endless moment, he opened his eyes. He was still standing on the ledge. The cliff had fallen only in his mind. Reluctantly, he looked down.

Valaren lay on the floor of the ravine, one leg twisted over a boulder. Aracco could not see his expression; he was too far away. Valaren looked small and still, like a broken casting. Hod and Taz were running toward him. Hod reached him first and bent over. He straightened up very slowly, his face like a round dark moon. Aracco shivered.

"He's dead," shouted Hod. His voice sounded hollow. The cliffs caught his words and flung them back. "Dead . . . dead . . . dead."

Aracco's fingers tried to bite into the cliff. *No!* he thought. *Hod's mistaken. I've got to get down there. Help Valaren.* Everything around him boomed and crashed, as if the cliff were truly falling. Dead . . . dead . . . dead . . . DEAD!

No! he thought again. *It isn't true.*

"Aracco!" Hod's voice reached him, a faint call through the avalanche inside his mind. "What should we do?" He looked down again. Taz was backing away from Valaren. Out of the corner of his eye he saw Emen sliding down his topline like a frightened monkey. Valaren still lay there, unmoving, on the ground below.

Climb down, he told himself. *Help Valaren.*

He looked down at his hands and realized they were shaking. "Get a rope!" he told Hod. He glanced across the cliff. Nago clung to the edge of the Beak, still trembling. His face looked ashen. "No, get two. Set toplines so Nago"—he spat out the name—"and I can get down. You, Emen, and you . . ." Aracco looked down at Taz. He was shivering so much he could hardly stand. He was in no shape to set lines. "Hod—help Emen."

He heard their voices climbing the path out of the ravine, then moving along the cliff top. He wished they would hurry. He had to get down. Get down fast. Fetch his mother—the healer—for Valaren. The

91

voices overhead blurred together. There was something wrong with his ears again. He heard a roaring like the Meged River in spring flood. *Another rockslide,* he thought. *Maybe the cliff is giving way. That's what happens when you go too deep. The climbers died. That's why they left the cliff.* A shadow swerved above him. "Eiroc!" he yelled. The ends of a rope came hissing past his shoulder.

Trembling, Aracco reached for his climbing iron. His fingers had clamped the stone so hard that his knuckles were pale—the color of bones. He clipped his climbing iron to the rope. He did not look down. A good climber seldom looks down.

He leaned back against the rope and started slowly down the cliff. *Hurry!* he told himself. He pushed off the cliff and bounded the rest of the way down, his feet hitting the stony sand at the bottom with a crunch. The roaring in his head stopped suddenly.

He unclipped his climbing iron, pushed the rope away, and stumbled toward Valaren. Very faintly overhead he heard the song of a meadowlark. He took a few more steps and knelt beside Valaren. He seemed to be asleep. Aracco put one hand on his friend's chest and shook him gently.

"Valaren," he whispered. "Wake up! Valaren?"

There was no response. Slowly Aracco became aware of the stillness underneath his hand. Valaren's body was warm, but no breath moved inside it. His friend was gone. Only an empty husk remained, brown eyes staring unseeing at the sky. Gently,

Aracco closed those eyes, freeing Valaren's spirit forever from his body. His fingers jerked back. He scrambled to his feet, shuddering, and gritted his teeth. In a moment he would be as useless as Taz. "Hod!" he snapped. "Get help. To the village. You and Emen. Take Taz!" Hod came down the cliff on the rope Aracco had descended and pulled Taz to his feet. Aracco watched them climb the path out of the ravine. Then he sank down beside Valaren's body, breathing hard into a sudden, blinding pain.

Valaren! he wanted to shout, but had no voice for it. *Why? Why were you a fool? Climbing to help Nago!*

And where is *Nago?* Bitterness filled his mouth. *Who cares! I hope he's on the cliff still. May an eiroc take him!*

Through his pain he heard the small sounds of pebbles falling, of a rope slapping against stone. He stared at the rocky sand beneath him, refusing to look up at the cliff. Then, hearing Nago's footsteps nearby, he squeezed his eyes shut.

Go away, he thought, *before I pound you into the sand.* The footsteps stopped beside Valaren's body, began again, receded. He could hear the lark clearly now, and the afternoon sun was warm on his shoulders. None of it mattered. Valaren was dead.

He sat there forever, aware of the rustling silence in the quarry, and the greater calm where Valaren's body lay. He dodged the thoughts that rose toward the surface of his mind. There was a dull ache in his head and he felt his blood throbbing in his ears. He alone stood vigil. Nago had disappeared. *Hiding,* thought Aracco bitterly. *As usual, he'll take no blame.*

After a while, he heard the voices of men from the village. He got to his feet, waiting.

Rad and Dolan approached with two of the journeymen, carrying a litter. They set it down and gathered around Valaren's body, standing with bowed heads. After a moment Dolan stepped back and slammed one fist into his palm.

"Young fools!" he cursed. "Climbing without toplines!" He gave Aracco an accusing glare. In his face Aracco saw a shadow of the old smith's praise for Valaren's skill. Never again would Valaren cast gold. Soon his ashes would be given to the River. Aracco felt himself sweating under Dolan's scrutiny.

It's not my fault! he wanted to shout. He ducked a rankling memory so quickly that it vanished deep inside his mind.

"Leave it, Dolan," Rad said firmly. "No need to mix blame with grieving."

The journeymen shifted Valaren's body onto the litter. Aracco walked behind them as the men climbed awkwardly out of the ravine, struggling to maneuver the litter along the narrow path. Rocks skidded under their feet and fell, crashing against boulders in the creek bed below. The echoes rang like gongs sounding for the feast of Barak. *The cliffs are honoring Valaren,* thought Aracco, then pushed the thought away with a grimace.

Valaren should not need to be honored. He should be alive!

A sharp image of Valaren climbing to Nago's aid flashed across his eyelids. Aracco winced. *If only I had* . . . He dodged the thought again. Radsmith was right.

A silent crowd met them in the village circle. Valaren's mother rushed to the litter, bending over her son's body. She raised her head, wailing a lament for her son. The other women joined in, their shrill voices keening with sorrow. All but Seri. She stood stone still, staring at her dead brother, her face blanched of all expression. Her silence stung Aracco. *Doesn't she care?* he thought. Keening women and weeping men surrounded him, but Seri's eyes were as dry as his own.

The sun rose above the eastern mountains, spilling its light over Meged. Aracco sat at the big oak table in his mother's house, his chin resting on his folded arms. The sweet bread on the table beside him was still untouched. He stared across the room at a long winding crack in the plaster wall. His gaze climbed the crack in the wall as a climber ascends a cliff, as Valaren had. . . .

He stood up abruptly, knocking over the stool. He didn't want to think about it, didn't want to remember. His father came into the room, his face deeply creased with lines of grieving.

"I am going to the crossroads now," Curran said

gently, "to help build the pyre. Will you come?"

Aracco nodded, trying to swallow the ache in his throat. Maybe when Valaren's body was burned, the image of his friend lying lifeless in the quarry would vanish with the smoke. He followed his father to the woodpile behind the house and began gathering branches into his arms. There seemed to be something wrong with his fingers. The wood kept slipping from his grasp. As he straightened up with a full load, his arms suddenly loosened and the wood clattered to the ground. He clenched his teeth and clumsily restacked his load, not daring to look at his father. He could feel tears at the back of his eyes. All it would take to make them fall was a gentle glance.

Aracco walked beside his father, carrying his burden toward the crossroads. Silence filled the space between them, but Aracco felt his father's grief as if it were his own. Their kinship bond—a deep unspoken understanding—held Aracco as if he was encircled by his father's arms. This was the feeling he'd been missing. But today he did not want it. Not like this! Not heavy with regret and pain. As they crossed the village circle, Curran spoke.

"I've been thinking about the mourning gift," he said softly. "Something Valaren's spirit would enjoy." Aracco felt tears rise suddenly in his eyes and scorch down his cheeks. He walked on, his arms full, unable to brush them away. Reaching the far side of the village circle, Aracco and his father started down a narrow street beside the inn.

"He was like the hala birds that travel the length of the River, endlessly curious," continued Curran, "and so I will give him a golden hala."

"Valaren," began Aracco, then choked on his friend's name. A small branch tumbled from his arms and bounced into the gutter. Aracco stared at it, trying to think of what to say. "Valaren would like a hala."

Why? he wondered, searching blindly through his misery for a reason. *What about it would Valaren like? Would it remind his spirit of the River? No, that wasn't right. It had to do with journeying.*

The street before him opened out onto the herders' road. At the crossroads, other boys and men were already gathered, building a pyre of logs and branches. Their greetings were subdued, tinged with sorrow. Curran added his gift of wood to the pyre, crossing the branches carefully so the flames would breathe freely. He looked over his shoulder at Aracco.

"Valaren wanted to be a trader."

"Yes, I know." Valaren had seen a way to satisfy his longing for adventure. He would have been a goldsmith and gone trading for the guild. He had seen his dreams of journeying beyond the trade routes as shining possibilities. But now Valaren would never seek Terenger, would never travel on the sea. Feeling numb, Aracco stacked his burden on the pyre.

When the pyre was finished, villagers gathered, bearing their mourning gifts. As Aracco took his place beside his father and mother, he saw Nago standing with the mastersmith. His fingers tightened on the golden mourning gift he held. He wanted to hurl it at Nago's sour face. But Valaren's passage mattered more than any feud with Nago. Aracco looked away, struggling to contain his rage.

Four of the smiths carried Valaren's body from the guildhall and laid it carefully atop the pyre. His body was draped in robes the color of flame.

Or the wings of a hala bird, thought Aracco. He felt hollow inside, empty as a walnut eaten by worms.

One by one the villagers went forward and laid their mourning gifts on the pyre. Many of them wept, tears of grieving rolling down their faces. Aracco saw Seri go forward. He stood very still, watching her. Her face looked as if it were carved from a brown stone upon which no light shone. She placed her gift of gold on Valaren's heart and retreated into the circle of mourners without a tear.

Doesn't she care? thought Aracco. *Doesn't she miss Valaren?* Her silence hurt him. He wished she would weep like the others. He thought that tears might be easier to bear. It was his turn now. Slowly, he stepped into the circle.

One foot forward, then another. He stared at the crossed branches, afraid to raise his eyes higher. When he could touch the soft red of Valaren's death robes, Aracco stopped. Heart pounding, he looked into his friend's quiet face. There was no mischief in it now. No smile gazed back at him from Valaren's warm brown eyes. Instead his eyes were closed, his eyelids masked with powdered gold. Aracco felt his throat close up until he could not breathe. With a gasp, he turned away, looking down at Valaren's lifeless chest, where a single piece of goldwork gleamed. Seri's gift.

It was a desert lion, so beautifully worked that he could hear its roar echo in his ears.

Did my father craft that? he wondered. Seri chose well. Her gift will remind Valaren of the desert. He stared at the golden lion, thinking of Valaren's last journey down the Great River to the camp of the Dahiri. Then he laid his own gift beside the lion. He had chosen a cloud leopard, the very first casting he had ever made, so that something of himself might travel with Valaren's spirit.

"All the way to the sea," he whispered. "May the River carry you." Looking into his friend's face for the very last time, he backed away from the pyre.

Others followed, until Valaren's body was outlined with goldwork. When all of the gifts had been given, Orin stepped forward and soaked the pyre with oil. Rad walked behind him, carrying a torch lit at the forging fire. He thrust it into the crossed branches and leaped back as the oil blazed.

Flames leaped up around Valaren's body. The funeral fire scorched the red robes, turning them to cinders. The fire licked Valaren's hair and then his face, until the skin began to blister and sear, withering. Cinders swarmed above the pyre like a cloud of gnats. Valaren's flesh fell away, devoured by the fire. A sweet stench hung heavy in the air. Bones blackened and cracked like the branches that fed the flames. The mourning gifts began to melt, and soon the branches of the pyre ran with dripping gold. Finally the pyre crumbled, burning slowly down to embers. When even the smoke had vanished, Jeron stepped forward and said the blessing for the dead.

"And from the embers, his spirit shall rise like the phoenix."

Aracco spoke the refrain without thinking, hearing the voices of the others from a great distance.

"And like the gold shall be reforged."

As the words died away, Valaren's mother and father stepped forward, each holding a large clay bowl. Aracco watched numbly. They sorted the melted gifts from the ashes, scooping the ashes into one bowl and the gold into another. Then Valaren's father covered the bowl of ashes and took leave of the village, bowing to the mastersmith and the crowd of mourners. He bowed finally to Seri, and at last, Aracco saw her tears. She wept without a sound. Aracco felt her pain sear into his soul, and it hurt so much he wanted to shout at her to stop weeping. Instead, he looked away, watching Valaren's father begin his journey to the Caracmeren, where all that remained of Valaren would be given to the River. The gold would be reforged. And Valaren's ashes would flow down the Great River to the sea.

Dusk shadowed the streets when Aracco left the smithy that day. Outside the open door of his mother's house, he paused, breathing in the earthy fragrance of the orchard. The peaceful strength of trees soothed the aching muscles in his arms and, gradually, began to ease the deeper pain inside his heart. A thrush sang, and its sweet song came pouring through him. Inside the house, he heard his mother and father speaking; her voice strong as thrush song, his voice as peaceful as the trees.

"Has Jeron decided?" his mother was saying.

Decided what? Aracco wondered. He began to listen, wrapping his arms across his chest against the evening chill.

"Yes." His father sounded hesitant. "I hope he understands the outcry it will cause. The noise will be heard in the guildhouse of Baraken."

"Very little escapes the mastersmith's notice," replied his mother. She chuckled. When she spoke again, her voice was soft and very tender. "But then, beloved man, why have you been teaching her if not for this?" Aracco moved closer, drawn toward the warmth of her love for his father.

"Not to would be a waste of a gift," Curran said.

"True enough," Kalisha agreed. She looked up at Aracco as he stepped through the doorway. He felt her strong gaze piercing through him.

"A gift," she added, "should be used as it is given."

What gift, wondered Aracco as he walked to the smithy the next morning, *does she think I should be using?* He had pondered her words and his parents' conversation late into the night. Having found no answers, he was still puzzling through the pieces. What did she mean? He had no idea what his gift might be, unless it was for climbing. Or for restlessness!

He reached the smithy and stood frowning up at the task slate. Under the leopard sign, the scribing smith had drawn a water bucket. Aracco shrugged. It could be worse. Out of habit, he looked to see where Valaren was assigned. Then he remembered. Valaren was dead.

Suddenly he ached all over, as if he, not Valaren, had fallen and somehow survived. Cursing, he picked up the buckets and hurried into the courtyard. They seemed heavier than usual as he pulled them out of the well. He stumbled crossing the courtyard, spilling some of the precious water into the dust and splashing his leggings. Aracco stopped, staring at the dark stain on the ground. In Caraccen, water was never wasted.

Does it matter? he thought, his misery so sharp that everything else seemed unimportant. *Let Jeron send me to the bellows!*

His shoulders hunched sharply at the thought of flames. He heard the roar of the pyre again and saw the cinders flapping overhead. Hurrying toward the casting room, he fled the memory.

He filled the troughs one by one, dimly aware of the subdued mood that filled the smithy. Even the apprentices were quiet at their tasks. Everyone was solemn, mourning for Valaren.

"Valaren's father is back," Hod whispered to Aracco that afternoon in the finishing room. Aracco stiffened, staring down at the red clay on his hands. The remembering feast would be held at sundown then. At the thought of it, the dull ache inside him sharpened. He curled his fingers in, covering his palms, as if that would somehow shield him from the pain. He didn't want to remember.

In the evening Aracco sat with the apprentices in the guildhall, listening numbly to the speeches. They were talking of some stranger who had died. No one he knew, that was certain.

"Kind and generous . . . A willing apprentice . . ."

The mild words washed over him. How absurd to speak that way about Valaren. What about the time he had filled all of the beekeeper's wax molds with honey? He turned to grin at his friend, but it was Emen who sat beside him. Valaren was dead, and the words they spoke for him were lifeless too. His grief rose into his throat until he could scarcely breathe. Clutching the edge of the table, he fought the images of Valaren's last climb. He saw his friend lying there, so far below. So still. So . . . dead. A shudder traveled slowly up his spine. Across the room, the master-smith rose to his feet.

"In a single day, our guild has lost two apprentices," said Jeron. "Gemmel, we believe, has gone to the goldcliffs. It is the first time since the guildhall at Meged was built that one of our apprentices has broken his vows. Valaren, although loyal to his guild, died the death of a climber. Tonight we remember Valaren."

Aracco swallowed hard. Despite the warmth in the guildhall, he was shivering. Behind his eyes he watched Valaren climb the Beak again. He pressed his fists against the table, willing this time to be different.

"Valaren was unusual among apprentices," the mastersmith continued, his cool voice pushing back the relentless image in Aracco's mind. "All apprentices rebel against the rulings of the guild, but Valaren asked questions that showed wisdom. He would not have been content to spend his days in the smithy, following traditions without reason. He had an urge to travel the Great River and learn new ways. Had he lived, he would have brought new wisdom to enrich our guild."

The mastersmith paused, bowing his head. A long, respectful silence filled the hall. When Jeron raised his head again, his face was stern; his mouth set in a thin, determined line. Aracco shuddered. He knew that look all too well. The mastersmith wore it when he sat in judgment, choosing fit punishment for unruly apprentices.

What will it be this time? thought Aracco, apprehensive. *Will he bar us from the quarry?* He dreaded that, despite Valaren's fall.

"I have been searching for an appropriate tribute . . ." said the mastersmith, "a way to honor Valaren." Aracco began to relax. Perhaps they would still be permitted to climb. "Tonight," Jeron continued, "I will name a new entrant in the contest, someone to whom Valaren would gladly bequeath his place."

Aracco stared at Jeron, outraged, deaf to the curious whispers around him. How could the master suggest such a thing? No one could take Valaren's place. No one!

Jeron raised his hand and the voices hushed.

"We have among us an apprentice whose passion for the gold is as strong as Curran's, an apprentice who that worthy smith predicts will someday surpass his skill."

Aracco bristled. *Outsmith my father? What apprentice could outsmith my father? Who would he praise so highly? Even for my finest work, I have never earned such praise.* He felt a sudden jealous anger toward this unknown rival. Glancing over at his father, he gained a gentle, rueful smile. *As if he knows I will never be that good,* Aracco thought. His heart felt bruised.

"In recognizing this apprentice," said Jeron, "our guild will honor what Valaren most cherished—a questioning heart." The mastersmith turned toward the side of the hall where Seri sat, her bright hair covered with a mourning veil, and bowed with a gentle elegance that stole Aracco's breath.

"Seri, beloved sister of Valaren, is that apprentice."

In stunned silence, Aracco watched Seri rise like a pale, uncertain flame. She walked toward the mastersmith, her steps uneven. He thought a single whisper might extinguish her, but as the murmurs began to rise and swarm like wasps, she held her head high and grew brighter.

"An outrage!" shouted someone. Aracco listened numbly as other voices buzzed throughout the hall.

"How dare the mastersmith defy tradition!"

"River save us!"

"What of the council?"

"They'll dissolve our hall!"

"First the eirocs, and now this!"

Jeron spoke again, his voice commanding. "Silence!" The single word cut through Aracco's numbness. He felt the edge of pain. All around him, voices stilled.

"Seri is hereby recognized as an apprentice of this goldsmiths' hall," declared Jeron. "She is named as an entrant in the contest for first apprentice. Curran has offered to stand as her guide."

Aracco stared at his father, disbelieving. Curran was grinning, leaning back in his chair and grinning. His expression stung Aracco even worse than Nago's scorn. *Is this what my father has been doing in his smithy?* he thought. *Teaching Seri to forge gold?* He did not want to believe it.

One by one, things he had not understood fell into place. Seri's hands powdered with red. Her threat to melt his bird. The conversation he had overheard the night before. Each was like a hammer blow inside him. His ears and face began to burn. Why had his father never told him? Why would he keep this secret from his only son? He turned toward his mother, seeking reassurance. But there was pride on her dark face, pride in Seri. She had known too.

Why? he longed to shout at them. *Why did you not tell me?* He felt as if his father's smithy door had been slammed in his face. And, with his pride in tatters, he wanted to be back inside.

"But, master!" someone shouted.

"Jeronsmith," argued Orin, "this goes against all tradition."

"A woman cannot be a goldsmith!" said Dolan, on his feet and snorting like an angry bull.

Jeron raised his hand again for silence. Scowling, Dolan sat down.

"When Barak b'Osiann taught the secrets of working gold to our ancestors," said the mastersmith, "a woman of the Osi worked at his side. The Osi teach their arts to man and woman alike. It is the goldsmiths who have strayed from tradition by barring women from the guild!"

"But women have not the strength," protested Dolan.

Aracco's father rose, his arms folded, unruffled by the crowd's indignation.

"Seri has both the skill and the strength," he said. "I have seldom seen an apprentice with the eagerness and quickness she possesses. She has a gift and will bring honor to our craft."

The words cut deep into Aracco's heart. *My father has never said as much of me,* he thought. He saw his father's familiar face, but the man who wore it was a stranger. The loneliness inside him was like a bitter wind. Off the mountains it came, shrieking of eirocs. He shivered, hugging his sides.

"But what of the council of smiths in Baraken?" said Orin.

"They know my work," replied Aracco's father.

"I will speak for Meged," said the mastersmith.

Aracco's mother rose gracefully. "The council elders are smiths," she said. "When they see her crafting, they will be swayed." Her voice was soft, but it carried as much strength and authority as Jeron's, soothing the crowd like healing balm. Even Aracco felt her gentle touch. The angry questions faded. A few tentative toasts were raised in Seri's honor. Valaren's sister stood by the mastersmith's table, her face bright and her hair escaping from its veil in tendrils of flame. Her brightness stung Aracco's eyes. *How can she take my place?* he wondered bitterly. *Beside my father. And Valaren's place in the contest.* He looked down at his plate, at the rinds and bones scattered on the gold. His hopes to gain his father's praise lay among the bones. Around him, he heard the sounds of people beginning to leave the hall. At the far end of the table, he heard Nago's voice taunting Chak.

"You haven't a chance, against a girl."

"Look to yourself, Nago," growled Chak.

"Seri!" Emen's voice broke through their quarrel. "Your brother would be proud." Looking up, Aracco saw her approaching their table. Emen leaned across it, heedless of the cups and plates, drawn to her like a lizard toward a patch of sunlight.

"Seri," Nago called, "let's see your muscles!"

Seri hesitated, the light in her face shadowed by his tone. Aracco sprang to his feet, snarling at Nago.

"Let her be!" The pain in him flared up into a blazing rage. This time, he would accept the challenge. It would feel grand to stuff his fist in Nago's mouth.

Nago retreated. Aracco watched, surprised and disappointed, as the mastersmith's son disappeared into the crowd. *Coward!* he thought. *Spineless one!*

Cursing Nago under his breath, he turned to look at Seri. Anger still burned behind his eyes. Why was she working at his father's side? The glow on her face flickered as she met his gaze.

"Aracco?" she said, her voice uncertain.

He glared at her. While he hauled charcoal and pumped the bellows, she'd been crafting gold in the little smithy. *It should be my place,* he thought angrily. *I'm his son!* Why had Seri won his father's praise?

"Why you?" he said, lashing out through his pain. "What makes you good enough?" Her face flushed, flaming bright again.

"You'll see, Aracco," she retorted. "I'll beat you!"

"And what about Valaren?" he demanded. "Don't you care?" He was shouting at her—he had to shout at someone.

She stared at him, sudden tears shining on her lashes.

"I thought you would be proud!" she said. Spinning around, she ran out of the guildhall.

Aracco walked home alone, jealousy still buzzing in his ears. Unlike himself, Seri truly wanted to craft gold. *My own father has been teaching her in secret,* he thought, *with my mother's blessing. And the mastersmith knew.* He still could not believe that Jeron, whose cold voice put the fear of guild rules in every apprentice, had flown in the face of tradition. And what about Valaren? Had Valaren known his sister's secret? That question hurt most him most of all, because his friend could never answer.

Curse it, Valaren. If you hadn't fallen. The hateful

image of his friend climbing toward Nago rose before him once again. He tried to blot it out. *If only I had* . . . He crushed the thought, afraid to face it. *It is Nago's fault, that rooster! Nago.* He hated Nago for everything. Aracco clenched his fists, wishing there was something he could smash.

As he passed the little smithy, he heard someone inside, weeping. The sobs tore into his angry thoughts and scattered them, leaving behind heaps of jagged pain. Seri . . .

He wanted to call her name, but he had no words. Grief and shame and jealousy were choking him. If only Valaren were here, she would have no cause to weep. He rushed into his mother's house and slammed the door.

Aracco woke blurrily the next day, with the confused feeling that something, he had forgotten what, was wrong. When he remembered, he groaned and stuffed his head beneath his pillow. Valaren—dead. And Seri—an apprentice. After last night, how could he possibly face her? He lay in bed, hiding from the day, until hunger and discomfort drove him out. When he stumbled into the main room, his mother looked up from sorting herbs at the table.

"Will you come gathering with me this morning?" she asked. "I need some more yarrow. I've sent word with your father to the smithy. They'll not be expecting you."

Aracco's relief was so intense it stung his eyes. He

nodded, not trusting his voice, and scooped up one of the seed cakes his mother had set out on the table. As he bit into it, he remembered tossing another seed cake to Valaren only two weeks before. He touched that day again, as real as the taste of the cake in his mouth. Eating slowly, he savored the memory.

When his meal was finished, Aracco followed his mother into the hills, carrying one of her gathering baskets. They wandered northeast from the village, looking for yarrow. The tall herb grew scattered in the grass, its gray-green fronds topped with clusters of white flowers. Aracco reached down when he saw it, pinched through the stem, and dropped the yarrow flowers in his basket. The smell of the bruised leaves made his nose wrinkle.

The morning sun warmed his face and the slow rhythm of gathering put him at ease. Times like these in the hills with his mother were always a welcome release from the smithy. Today he felt the sensations like a strong poultice, slowly drawing out his pain. From a nearby clump of oaks, a dove called softly. As he walked along, pausing now and then to pick the yarrow, dry grass swished against his legs.

"This is worth doing," he said, watching his mother's dark hands pluck another crown of yarrow. "Everything around us is so much alive. Not like working gold. What does Seri see in it?"

As he spoke her name, he felt a stab of jealousy.

His mother glanced over at him. "A path she would follow. Your father's path. Seri loves working the gold as much as he does. But what of you, my son? What is it that you want?"

Aracco shrugged, turning away from her. Why even ask? He was bound by his vows to be a smith's apprentice. Even if Seri had stolen his place. He looked across the tawny hills. Beyond them rose the shining, distant mountains. His spirit soared to greet them.

"To climb!" he said impulsively. "To climb those mountains!"

Kalisha smiled. "Seeking Terenger?" she asked. "That I cannot grant you. You must ask Jeron, your master. But think on my words, Aracco. Turn your heart toward finding your path, and let your father and Seri follow their own."

My path? thought Aracco. *What path is that? All I know is that I want adventure. And Jeronsmith would say no.*

Scowling, he tugged at his shoulder strap until the basket rested on his hip again. He worked beside his mother, matching his stride to her own. The rhythm of the day caught hold of him again. Grass bowed before him, and all around, bird songs soared. He felt his mother's peaceful strength and beneath him, even greater, the vital power of the earth. He felt in harmony, at one with life around him. But the question of his own path persisted, echoing inside his mind.

Path, what path? Climber, herder, Terenger . . . He tried to shrug it off. He had no idea of what his path might be. All he really knew was that the smithy seemed too small.

"There now, that's enough," his mother said at last. "We'll return by the herders' road. I promised Seri I would bring her some sheeproot. Her arms are sore from striving so hard in the smithy. She truly hopes to win the contest."

Aracco's fingers clamped down on his basket, crushing the herbs.

"Why does *she* want to win?" he demanded. "Is it not enough to be the first woman apprenticed since the days of Barak?"

"It is her way of honoring Valaren," said Kalisha. "Can you not see this, my son? When the flamebrush turns brown and drops its seed, all the tears of autumn cannot free the life inside. Fire is needed to crack the hard shell and open a path for the rain. Only then can the new plant grow. Seri has chosen the path of fire."

Aracco shook his head, refusing to look at his mother. Her words rang in his head, but they made no sense. What did flamebrush seeds have to do with Valaren?

And who did Seri think she was? Resentment burned inside him. He could find no real answer to his mother's question, but he was certain of one thing. When the day came, he would win the contest and his father's praise. He'd show Seri her place!

*W*hen *Aracco entered the forging room that after*-
noon, he heard Seri's light voice asking someone a
question. Hunching his shoulders against her presence, he took his place at the benches. On the edge of
his vision, he saw her working beside Rad, turning a
hot bar of gold while the smith beat it smooth. Seri's
hair was the color of fire. Her bare arms looked
strong from the days of working with his father. Already, she seemed at home in the smithy.

But she doesn't belong here! he thought. *Valaren
should be here, not his sister.* Picking up a hammer,
he sought refuge in his task: shaping the cup he was
beating out from sheet gold.

Clunk, clunk, *clang.* Soon, he found a singing
rhythm to the gold. *Clang,* clang, clang. Some of the
peace he had felt in the hills with his mother stayed

with him through the afternoon, making the work flow. It even eased a little the discomfort he felt when he saw Seri standing where she had no right to be.

That night his dreams were haunted, filled with cinders and shrieking birds, images of death. Clouds shrouded the sun as he crossed the smithy courtyard the next morning. The forging room was like a gloomy cave. Seeing Emen at the bellows, Aracco frowned, trying to remember the signs on the task slate. He was certain it had not been Emen's turn. Too numb with misery to ask, he sat down at the bench to finish his cup. He picked up the handle he had cast, turning it in his hands. Two swans adorned it, their slender necks twining up its curve. A brighter mood touched him as he held the swans, as if the sun outside was piercing through the clouds. They were beautiful; strong and full of grace. Today he would meld them to the cup and see their beauty honored.

Melding was difficult. The joining edges of the gold had to be heated until they softened, but kept from the heat point where the gold would lose its shape. Rad had taught him to watch the color of the gold so he would know just the right moment to remove it from the fire. He picked up the cup and walked over to the forge. Emen looked up from tending the bellows as Aracco chose the tongs he needed from the rack. Emen's eyes seemed half focused, like those of a sleeper waking from a dream.

Aracco shuddered, trying to shake off the lingering

shadows of his own dreams. Clenching a pair of tongs in each hand, he extended the cup and its handle into the flames. He rested his elbows on the stone edge of the forge. Gradually, the gold began to turn red. Flame red, like Valaren's death robes. Valaren had been good at melding. Shoving the thought away, Aracco turned the tongs that held the cup. He had to focus on the work; that was the art of melding.

Remembering Rad's instructions, he turned the cup slowly. "A good meld should be blended so that even a smith cannot see the join." Like a climber who becomes part of the stone. Just as Nago had been melded to the cliff.

Aracco jerked the cup and handle out of the fire, glaring down at them. He didn't want to think about Nago! Or Valaren! Only the work. He had to concentrate, to be as single-minded as a climber, if he wished to win the contest.

I have to win, he thought, returning the cup and handle to the flames. *I have to beat Seri. If it means giving up climbing and sitting all day in the smithy like Chak, I'll do it. If Valaren were here, there would be no need, but now . . .*

Aracco swore under his breath, staring unwillingly once again at Valaren's death. Valaren peeling off the cliff. Valaren lying there, unmoving, on the floor of the ravine. His empty face, brown eyes staring up at nothing. Valaren's lifeless body, shrouded in red.

He heard a soft hiss and focused his eyes in alarm. The cup had slumped. Gold dripped into the fire.

117

Aracco stared at it, horrified. Again he saw melted gold running down the branches of Valaren's pyre. Jerking the ruined cup and handle out of the flames, he dumped them, tongs and all, into the cooling trough and fled the smithy.

Outside in the alley, he felt better. The clouds had moved away and sunlight warmed the air. Aracco took a deep breath. He glanced at the smithy, then turned his back on it. He'd face the consequences later.

"Hey, Daki! Where are you going?"

Aracco spun around, his hands closing into fists. The name *Daki* insulted anyone akin to the Dahiri tribes. He glared at the mastersmith's son, who stood behind him, sneering.

"What's it to you, Nago?" he demanded.

Scorpion! he thought. *Mock my mother's people once more and I'll squash you.* Nago took a step forward and shrugged, his wiry shoulders making an insult of the gesture. Aracco hated his face; you could never tell what he was thinking. Nothing pleasant, that was certain.

"I thought you'd be in the smithy, that's all," said Nago. "Now that Seri's in the contest."

Anger rumbled in Aracco's chest. *I've got to win,* he thought. *But what does Nago care?*

"What of you?" he demanded, at that moment remembering who should have been at the bellows. "Shirker!"

"Big words," Nago scoffed, "from one sneaking off to go climbing."

"Report me to your father then. Telltale!"

Challenge glittered in Nago's eyes. "We'll just see who wins the contest. It won't be you, Aracco." He spit into the dust. "Horsehands!"

Flaming mad, Aracco charged. He crashed to the ground with Nago beneath him. Dust rose, making him cough. He found his breath and smashed his fist into Nago's chin. The pain felt good. Nago would feel it more. An elbow ground into Aracco's ribs. He clenched his jaw and struck again. His knuckles burned. His ear was stinging from a blow. He rolled and dug his elbow into Nago's stomach.

The air was full of dust. He tasted blood and twisted out from under Nago's flailing arm. Breathing in short gasps, his nostrils full of Nago's sour smell, Aracco aimed for his enemy's nose.

Strong hands gripped Aracco's shoulder and pulled him to his feet. His fist swung uselessly through empty air. Dusty and panting, he stood glaring down at Nago. Eyes wide, the mastersmith's son scrambled up and backed away. Uneasily, Aracco turned his head. The long-fingered hand clamping hard on his shoulder wore the guildhall's seal. With a shudder, he shook off the hand and turned around. Planting his feet in the dust, he raised his eyes to stare defiantly at the mastersmith.

"Who struck first blow?" Jeron's cool voice cast a chill on the morning. His gold-trimmed tunic was untouched by the dust that sifted down Aracco's neck. Aracco clenched his teeth to keep from shivering. He threw back his shoulders.

119

"I did." He braced himself, waiting for the master-smith's judgment. What would it be? A week at the bellows?

The mastersmith stared down at him. As usual, a stern expression masked his narrow face. But, for a moment, Aracco thought he glimpsed compassion in the master's eyes. The silence lengthened until he thought he could not bear it any longer.

"I'll not have my apprentices brawling like Baraken street boys," Jeron said finally. "Do you understand, Aracco? One more fight and I'll bar you from the contest."

Nago took a step forward. Aracco saw him smirking.

Coward! he thought. *Nago never takes full blame. And his father never judges him as harshly.* Aracco folded his arms and glowered at Jeron, who stared back, cool as polished gold.

"You were going climbing?" said the mastersmith. "Very well, Aracco. Go then, with my leave."

Aracco stared, astonished, as the mastersmith turned toward his son. Leave? When the mastersmith knew full well he'd left the smithy without it?

He saw Nago's smirk vanish abruptly as his father's hand clamped down on his shoulder. The mastersmith steered his son back toward the smithy. Aracco watched them disappear inside. Then he turned on his heel and began striding up the alley. He gritted his teeth, angry that Jeronsmith had blamed him for the fight.

It was Nago's fault, that rooster! I'd like to pull his feathers. Suddenly, he laughed out loud. He'd been given leave to climb by the mastersmith himself! And Nago, at the very least, would be back at the bellows. On the herders' road, he lengthened his stride. Summer dust stirred under his feet. A breeze whispered through the poplar trees and bitterbrush that veiled the river. Ripples of tawny grass spread across the hills. A rosy jay jeered from a nearby oak, reminding him of Nago. His bruises were beginning to ache. Remembering the mastersmith's warning, he groaned. Bar him from the contest? But he had to win! He would stay away from Nago, then. Until after the contest.

In the quarry, he chose a familiar route up the goldcliff, one not too close to the Beak. The stone under his hands felt soothing and solid. He let his mind flow into the rock and followed its lines up the cliff.

When the sun stood overhead, hunger gnawed, spoiling his sense of rhythm. He pulled himself into the shade of the cliff top oaks and started back toward Meged.

In the smithy courtyard, the apprentices were eating their noon meal. He was relieved to see that Seri was not with them. Chak was missing too, but Nago was there, sitting apart from the others on the far side of the well. Aracco collected his share of the meal and settled down among the younger boys.

"Where have you been?" Emen asked, his forehead wrinkled with concern. "Radsmith asked for you." Aracco pushed his fingers through his sweat-damp, curly hair and grinned. "Climbing!" The other boys stared. Hod's jaw dropped, his stolid face startled into motion. Across the courtyard Nago raised his head. Aracco braced himself, waiting for the stab of Nago's tongue, but the mastersmith's son looked down again, saying nothing.

"How can you bear it?" whispered Taz. He stared at Aracco, blinking rapidly, his hands moving in bewildered circles. Taz had been almost useless in the smithy lately. He seemed completely lost without Valaren.

"I couldn't bear not to," said Aracco. "But I won't be going again. Not until after the contest." The words felt heavy somehow, tasting unpleasant on his tongue. To strengthen his resolve, he glared at Nago.

Nago looked up, staring back at him with shadowed eyes. Aracco tensed, waiting for a challenge. To his amazement, Nago dropped his gaze and looked away. *Barak's law!* thought Aracco, feeling satisfied. *Jeronsmith's judgment must have been harsh to keep that rooster silent.* For once it seemed Nago had taken his share of the blame.

The clappers sounded, summoning them back to their tasks. Rad looked up from the forge as Aracco came into the room, but said nothing about the ruined cup. The handle, Aracco realized, picking it up from his bench where someone had set it, was unharmed. He chose a fresh sheet of gold and began the slow task of beating out a new cup. Now that he had decided to give up climbing, the work seemed easier. All around him hammers rang. The noise was like a pulse, the life of the smithy. Pounded smooth, forged in fire, and hammered out again. *This is my path,* he told himself firmly, closing his mind to the goldcliff and the eastern mountains. *I will prove worthy of my father's praise!*

At midafternoon, Chak passed through the forging room with a message for the smith. When he had given it, Rad raised his hand for silence. The apprentices laid down their hammers. "Tonight, by Jeron's decree," the smith announced, "there will be a gathering fire." Taz leaned toward Aracco, his face brightening for the first time since Valaren's death.

"That means stories," he whispered.

Aracco nodded bleakly, sharing none of the other boy's excitement. He'd as soon not go. Valaren had loved the gathering fires as much as Taz did, or more. Tonight the circle would feel empty.

At sundown, a gathering fire was kindled in the village circle. A few at a time, the villagers settled around it, until all of Meged was there. Gathering was a time for stories and musing among friends, a time for casting out thoughts that troubled the thinker. There were many voices raised around Aracco. He heard talk of eirocs and the threat to the goldcliffs. Of Gemmel and Valaren. Fears and sorrow, being spoken, were released and offered to the flames. But tonight Aracco found no comfort in the fire. It brought images of the pyre, of Valaren's body withering. He looked away and met Seri's gaze. She gave him a tentative smile. Still angry with her, Aracco scowled and turned to face the darkness. Behind him, scraps of legend were being drawn from the fire on the voices of old men.

"In Terenger, the streets are made of gold."

"They say there's gold enough to gift the River for a hundred years."

"Someone should seek Terenger."

I would go, Aracco thought, *if I had leave.* He fought the sudden urge that rose to meet this thought. There was his father's praise and the contest to win. The old men's tales flowed around him like a restless wind.

"In Terenger, they have small, swift boats like those of the wizardfolk, and they journey on the sea."

"They say that, in Barak's day, men passed freely from Caraccen to Terenger. Caravans carried trade goods from the sea people to the wharves of the Great River."

"Over the mountains?" asked Emen. "How could any herdbeast climb the cliffs?"

A man could, thought Aracco, *a climber could.*

"Not over, through. The Osi tunneled a passage through the mountains. Before the eirocs came."

"Do you hear that, Hod?" said Taz. "There's a tunnel to Terenger."

A tunnel, thought Aracco. *Valaren, do you hear? A*

road to Terenger. Staring into the night, he was filled with thoughts of his friend, until every part of him was aching, mourning for Valaren, who would never cross the mountains. And mourning for himself as well, caged inside the smithy.

"And there's a road to Baraken." Nago sneered. "Do you believe everything you hear, Tassy? Streets of gold, what oredust."

Aracco swung around in time to see the brightness snuffed from Taz's face. Nago was gloating. Flames began rising in Aracco's head; he felt the war rage of his desert kin burning in his veins. He saw Valaren's face, heard his friend's voice saying, "I would like to find a way there." Inside Aracco, something snapped. He sprang to his feet.

"Valaren believed it!" he spat at Nago. "He believed the streets are gold! And I will prove it true." People turned to stare at him, but he held his ground, glaring down at Nago.

"Will you really?" Taz burst out. "Cross the mountains?"

Nago shrugged as if Aracco's vow was a breath of bad air. "Don't get excited, Taz." His eyes narrowed, considering Aracco. "They say that Daki have short tempers and shorter memories. He'll forget his oath by morning!"

Aracco stiffened. In his mind he heard Dahiri warriors yell. He had sworn it. A Dahiri kept his word!

"In the morning," he vowed, "I leave for Terenger! I will not return until I find the golden streets." He

125

drew a breath, aware that everyone in Meged was listening now, and searched for words to equal his resolve. "In Barak's name," he said, "I swear it!"

As soon as he had spoken, Aracco knew why Nago goaded him. The contest. Inside him, the flames burned even hotter, fanned by Nago's grinning face. He wanted to spring on Nago, tear the triumph from his face.

Say something! he thought. *Give me an excuse to fight. Now it matters little if Jeronsmith bars me from the contest. Tomorrow I am leaving Meged.*

For the mountains! Excitement rushed in, quenching his rage. *I've found it!* he thought. *A way to leave the smithy. And to return again with honor.* His vow, spoken in Barak's name, might be strong enough to free him from the bonds of his apprenticeship.

"But, Aracco," Seri cried, "you'll miss the contest!" Her distress only heightened his rising sense of freedom. When he stood in Terenger, he would not care who wore the badge of first apprentice. He faced the crowd, but in his mind he saw the eastern mountains. Mountains he would climb!

"But the eirocs!" Hod protested.

Aracco gritted his teeth. He had forgotten all about the eirocs.

"Many have tried to cross the mountains," murmured Orin, "but not one has returned."

Aracco raised his chin. *I will return,* he vowed. *With gold, so that Meged has no lack.* Across the fire he saw his father's eyes upon him. *When I come home again my father will be proud. I will free Meged from its fears. With gold from Terenger!*

"Mastersmith," asked Rad, "will you allow this foolishness?" Everyone's attention shifted toward Jeron. The mastersmith rose and faced the gathering.

"Aracco has sworn an oath in Barak's name," he said. "I will not prevent his leave-taking. Meged has need of a new source of gold. But I lay upon him the charge to finish his apprenticeship when he returns." Aracco braced himself under Jeron's stern gaze. "Do you understand, Aracco? You still owe your duty to the guild. Even if you fail to find the golden streets, as master of this guildhall, I command you to return to Meged when your quest is finished."

"If he is not birdfeed," muttered Dolan.

Aracco was silent. Eirocs or no, if he failed, what reason would he have to return? His father would have no cause for pride. And Nago would torment him forever.

"If you will not agree to this," Jeron said evenly, "I will chain you to the bellows until you are a journeyman."

Aracco glowered at the mastersmith. "I will return," he said reluctantly. Everyone was watching him, and he felt a fool.

"Good journeying, then," said Jeron, granting Aracco one of his rare, brilliant smiles. "We will feast on your return."

11

Aracco set his empty pack on the big oak table. He folded his cloak and shoved it into the pack. He felt torn this morning, impatient to be off, but reluctant to be going. Last night's excitement was overshadowed by the painful thought of leaving everyone he knew.

His mother came swiftly into the room and dumped a pile of woolen clothing on the table. She was angry; he could tell by the sharp edges in the way she moved. She vanished into the cookery without a word.

Why? Aracco thought. *She wanted me to choose a path. Well, now I've chosen one.* This morning, however, he was not so certain. Was it foolishness to try and cross the mountains? Feeling glum, he packed his clothing.

"Aracco?" He looked up, frowning. Seri stood in the front doorway, clutching a climbing iron. Her face was stone smooth, hiding her feelings. Taking several steps into the house, she held out the climbing iron.

"Take it," she pleaded. "Please. It's Valaren's." Aracco's chest tightened. Slowly, he reached out to take the joined rings of metal. Valaren's climbing iron. He wanted to say something gentle, to thank her for the gift. But as he took the climbing iron, his hand brushed her fingers. Fire burned along his arm and set his heart aflame. His words were swept away. Seri jumped back as if she'd been stung.

"Good journeying," she whispered, and fled outside.

Aracco hurried to the door, his heart still pounding. "Seri," he called, "wait!" She turned, poised on her toes like a skittish young lamb. He stared at her, amazed. Had he ever seen her clearly? "I hope," he said. "I hope you win the contest!"

Seri flushed. Her brown eyes glistened. "You've made it easier," she snapped, "by going." Her face paled and she spun around, darting up the road. Aracco watched her running, her red hair shining bright as tears, until she disappeared around the bend. Then, rubbing his hand, he went back to the table. What had he meant to say? Something gentle, something brave. But Seri's touch had been so . . . strange. Feeling shaken, he tucked Valaren's climbing iron in his leather pack.

His mother reappeared, her hands full of summer-fruit. Aracco took the smooth red fruit and set it gently in the pack on top of his leggings. Turning away without a word, Kalisha rummaged in her wooden chest. A mournful wind rose inside Aracco as he watched her. He would miss her wisdom when he reached the mountains. Why was she angry? Hearing a sound, he looked up and saw his father standing in the doorway.

His father. A familiar round face with slanting brows, half smiling as he watched Kalisha. His father, whose praise he longed to gain. His father whom he hardly knew at all.

"Kalisha?" Curran said, his voice warm with love and humor. "Are you still silent?"

At his words, Aracco felt his mother's tension rising like a gale. Her skirts flared as she straightened up and spun around. He raised his hands, shielding himself from her anger.

"Is this a path you have chosen?" she demanded. "Or do you merely run from choosing? May Osiann the Elder shape good of it. Be careful not to stumble on your pride, my son! The mountains are not gentle."

Suddenly the anger died out of her eyes. Reaching across the space between them, she offered him a healer's kit—packages of herbs and healer's tools in a soft leather bag. When she spoke again, her voice was calm. "My dreams say you may have need of this. Good journeying, my son."

"We will walk with you to the crossroads," added

his father. Coming forward, he laid his warm hand on Aracco's hair. "I will miss you, my beloved son." Aracco felt the words flow into him with all the strength and gentleness his father used in crafting gold. The ache inside him lessened, his resentment toward Seri fading. Did it really matter whom his father chose to guide?

I'm still his son, Aracco thought, *his only child.* He heard the heartbeat of his father's love, deep and steady, like the rhythm of his hammer through the little smithy's open door. Would it really falter if he chose not to be a smith?

His father's hand withdrew. Aracco closed the pack and pulled its straps over his shoulders. He stepped through the doorway and started down the road, his parents following. Looking back, he saw them walking with their arms entwined and felt another pang. Was it right, this path of leaving?

As they passed the smithy, the younger apprentices crept out of the doorway and fell into step beside Aracco. There was no sign of Nago, or of Seri. Aracco felt disappointed. Her absence caused a silent space that all of Taz's chatter could not fill.

I wanted to see her again, he thought, then pushed away the thought and squared his shoulders. *When I return from Terenger,* he told himself, *she will be proud.* He turned his back on the smithy and tried to focus on what Taz was saying.

". . . when you get to Terenger. Oh, Aracco, just think!"

When I return from Terenger, he thought, *Seri will*

dance in my honor. He imagined himself, sitting at the head table beside the mastersmith and watching Seri dance. Remembering the way she moved, his ears grew hot.

At the crossroads Aracco turned, facing his mother and father and friends. His chest tightened again. He wanted to leave quickly, yet he was unwilling to go. "Stay in the River's blessing," he said.

"And go with the River's grace," replied his father, "on whatever path you follow." Curran's steady hand rested on Aracco's shoulder. His warm smile was as precious as his praise.

"Climb well," his mother added. "Go swiftly and come back with good speed." Her dark eyes held his gaze. Their depths offered courage and a warning, reminding him of the words she had spoken in anger.

"May your hands touch gold," said Emen. He was standing taut again, his thin face haunted by too many losses. Aracco clasped his hand.

"Courage, Emen," he said, "I too will land on my feet." Gemmel's brother gave him a grateful smile.

"Think of the stories when you return!" said Taz. His enthusiasm was so contagious that Aracco grinned, the thought of leaving seeming much less grim. Last, he turned toward Hod.

Hod held out his hand and dropped a white lumestone into Aracco's palm. "For the tunnel," he said.

The lumestone was Hod's most prized holding, a small round stone that glowed with its own pale light. A wizard stone, Hod called it, and said it granted visions. Aracco swallowed hard.

"Are you certain, Hod?" he whispered.

Hod nodded, his face solemn. "Take it, and good journeying."

With a last look at each of their faces, Aracco started up the herders' road. His footsteps dragged at first, but once past the quarry, he felt light-footed and relieved. Step by step his troubles shrank and vanished in the dust behind him. He felt light, like a bird. Joy rose inside him until he wished he truly had wings. Nago had tricked him into his vow, but now this quest seemed better than any honor given by the guild. And when he got to Terenger and saw the streets of gold, he would feel worthy of his father's name. He watched the road before him, eager for glimpses of the eastern mountains.

In the late afternoon, he left the road and cut across the grassy hills. The herders' road wandered south for many leagues, and he sought a quicker way to the mountains. In the distance he could see the dark green haze that marked the forest. With luck, he would reach the trees tomorrow evening. Curiosity quickened his footsteps. He had only been there once before, to the lower edges where the sawyers of Meged cut pines for building. Even then he had wanted to climb higher.

Just before nightfall he found a sheltered hollow where a stream flowed, crossing his path as it wandered toward the Meged River. Taking off his pack, he pulled out waybread and goat cheese. The salty cheese would last a day or two, and then he would have to hunt for his meals. When he had eaten, Aracco spread his cloak on the ground and sheltered in its folds. For a while he lay awake, looking peacefully up at the stars. That night he dreamed of Terenger, of golden streets beside a shining sea.

Dusk was coming fast when he reached the forest on the second day. The old pine trees stood well apart and there was little brush to hinder him. He walked quickly through the shadows, seeking water. Beside the whisper of a tiny spring, he slept soundly, wrapped in his cloak. In the morning, after feasting on waybread and summerfruit, he set off again, taking deep breaths of the fragrant air. All around him rose the tortoiseshell trunks of the pines. The ground rose steadily beneath his feet. With each stride, Nago and the smithy and Valaren's ashes fell farther behind. When a red and yellow tanager bounced whistling along a pine bough, Aracco whistled back.

But for bird songs and small rustling noises in the brush, it was quiet in the forest. By the fourth day, Aracco heard a ringing in his ears when he stood still, as if he stood in the smithy when all the hammers were silenced at once. Images of Meged returned to trouble him. Huddled in his cloak that night, a little hollow in the stomach after his first sparse meal, he felt the whisperings of loneliness. He curled around his pack and closed his eyes, thinking of Valaren.

Is it true what the deathwords say? he wondered.

Will his spirit be reforged? Seeking company, he sifted through memories of his friend until he fell asleep.

On the fifth day of his journey he reached the upper ranges of the forest. The trees grew more scattered here and he found himself on the edge of a wide meadow. A warm tongue of wind licked his face. He thought of the forging fire and the bellows and breathed out a contented sigh. This was far better than sweating in the smithy!

"Gold!" Aracco shouted to the rosy jay perched squawking in a nearby pine. "In Terenger the streets are gold!" His bare legs brushed the grass as he strode across the meadow. The afternoon heat pressed against his skin. It reminded him of the bellows again, and of Nago's scorn. He thrust his shoulders back against his leather pack.

It's not just a tale for old men, he thought fiercely. *I'll prove Nago wrong and stuff his mouth with golden pebbles!*

A warning hiss brought him to a sudden halt, poised on the balls of his feet. He watched a dust-colored snake ripple through the grass and disappear. Aracco let his breath out slowly. "Go in peace, death-bringer," he whispered. Fearing the snake as an omen, he scanned the sky above the meadow. The only bird to be seen was the jay, which left its perch and swooped across the clearing. Aracco shook off his apprehension and regained his stride, glancing now and then up at the sky.

When he entered the shade of the pines at the

upper edge of the meadow, his feet fell silently on dusty ground. Chill air began to gather in the shadow of the trees. He pulled his leggings out of his pack and put them on. As he shouldered his pack, he noticed its lightness. It was time to think about hunting for food.

Late that afternoon, when Aracco heard erratic movements in the brush, he crouched down swiftly, reaching for the slingshot in his belt. He waited, breathing softly as a brown hare hopped into the open, its long ears flickering. Aracco slipped a stone into the leather sling.

The hare sat back on its powerful hind legs, nose trembling as it tested the air. Aracco shifted his weight and released the sling. A twig snapped under his heel. The hare leaped toward shelter. Aracco sent a second stone flying after the first.

The hare tumbled head over tail, caught by death in midleap. Aracco sprang forward, bending over its warm, limp body. He touched its forehead.

"Fleet of foot, long-eared brother," he whispered. "Thank you for the life you give to feed me." He cleaned the hare with his knife and buried its entrails in the duff beneath a tree. Then Aracco swung the dead hare over his shoulder and moved up through the forest, looking for a place to camp. Around him, the sunlight had faded into shadows and his ears felt nipped by the air. Hearing water chattering, he hurried toward the sound.

A boulder-strewn riverbed dwarfed its narrow stream. Climbing down the bank, Aracco filled his water flask and stood up, staring at the peaks above him. They glowed pink and gold with sunset, but the dark air overhead seemed full of secrets. Again, he searched the sky for eirocs. Nothing moved on wings. Whistling a smithy tune, Aracco picked his way upstream. Maybe the eirocs had left the mountains.

He built his fire in a sandy hollow of the riverbed and began to roast the hare. Pulling waybread and a summerfruit from his pack, he remembered his mother's dark eyes as she bid him good journeying. He bit into the summerfruit, staring at the crackling flames. What were they doing now, his mother and father? Did Seri sit at the big oak table, breaking pieces off a seed cake and chattering about her day in the smithy? As the images of home filled his mind, he felt a hollowness in his stomach that had little to do with hunger.

He turned the hare on its spit, longing instead to be in his mother's house, surrounded by the smell of herbs. The room would be warm from the day's baking and filled with an oil lamp's glow. And his father would be there, the peace in his eyes deep after a day of smithing. A little remote, so at one with his work that he seemed always to be listening to a sound Aracco could not hear. The rhythm of a hammer, maybe, or the song of gold. Aracco tossed the summerfruit pit into the darkness and lifted the roasted hare off the fire. Perhaps when he had eaten, he would not feel so much alone.

When his hunger was satisfied, he banked the fire

with stones. He wrapped the carcass and the rest of the meat in the goat-cheese cloth and himself in his woolen cloak. A thin moon rose over the eastern mountains. He lay awake, gazing at the stars.

A sudden clatter of pebbles fell from the riverbank. Aracco sat up, staring into the night. For a long time he waited, hearing nothing more. Then, near at hand, he heard the faint whisper of footpads upon stone. It was a heavy, slightly clumsy sound. Aracco thought of bears and crept swiftly toward his fire. Removing the stones, he added kindling and tried to coax a flame from the coals. The sticks began to smoke. He blew gently on the new flames, glancing up from the tiny fire to stare into the darkness surrounding his camp. His heart thudded and his hands felt cold.

By Barak, he thought, *if only the moon were bigger.*

Sand rustled under heavy, uncertain feet. A flicker of movement caught his eye. Then a long, lean shape emerged from the night, and paused, wary of the crackling fire. Pale fur glinted between spots of darkness.

A cloud leopard! thought Aracco, his heart lurching in his chest. Sign of his father's house and most elusive of hunters. His fear was mixed with awe and admiration. What, in Barak's name, had called a leopard to his camp? The cloud leopard raised her head. He saw his fire burn, reflected in her hungry eyes.

Aracco reached for his knife.

The leopard blinked. Released from her blazing eyes, Aracco saw that her jaw was full of quills and swollen. The light from his fire cast deep shadows on her hollowed sides. He settled back on his heels, his heartbeat slowing. The leopard had challenged a spiny pig. Now she was starving. Pity washed over him, flowing into the place of his fear. Slowly, so as not to startle the leopard, he reached for his pack and drew out the healer's kit.

Keeping one eye on the leopard, Aracco took out a pair of thorn-pullers and set them down, then searched through the leather bag for the herb he needed. Finding a packet of comfrey, he mixed it with water in his cooking pot and set it on the fire. Now he was ready. As he picked up the thorn-pullers again, his fingers tightened on the cold metal. What he was about to do was folly, but how could he not attempt it? He had learned too much of his mother's healing art to ignore her teachings. Murmuring Dahiri words of friendship, he crawled slowly toward the leopard.

The sand beneath him whispered with his fears. What if cloud leopards did not know the Dahiri tongue? The she-leopard's jaws might be swollen shut, but her claws were sharp enough to kill. He might be a fool indeed to expect gratitude from a starving leopard.

The leopard's ears flickered and Aracco paused, his heart hammering. He was close enough now to see her flanks shivering with fever. Taking a deep breath, he tried to strengthen his resolve. The leopard was in pain, and he had been given the tools of a healer. Once again, he crept forward until he was almost within striking range. The leopard crouched on her haunches, tail quivering. Aracco spoke again, very softly, hoping his voice would not show fear.

"I come in peace," he whispered. "Let there be friendship between us. Let Osiann know us together in friendship." He slid one hand across the sand, then drew his knee forward. The leopard's tail twitched a warning. Aracco paused again, holding his breath as he watched her warily. Her tail swished once more and curled around to rest against her bony sides. Taking a very deep breath, Aracco crept into the striking circle of her claws.

"With these," he said, extending the thorn-pullers

for the leopard to smell, "I will pull out the spiny pig's thorns." He felt the leopard's breath touch his hand briefly and withdraw. Her tail was silent.

Offering a prayer to Osiann the Elder, Aracco grasped the first of the quills. The leopard jerked back, a growl rising in her throat. Her tail beat an angry rhythm on the sand.

"Be patient, my sister," pleaded Aracco. "The quill is out! You must let me pull the others." Slowly, her tail quieted, but not until it rested on the sand did he find the courage to reach for the second quill. Even then, it was hard to keep his hand from trembling. Thinking of his mother's hands when she worked as a healer, he willed himself to have the same calm certainty. One by one he removed the quills, keeping an eye on the cloud leopard's tail. The tip twitched slightly each time he grasped a quill and drew it out, but otherwise the she-leopard was still.

By the time he pulled out the last of the quills, his fingers were shaking with weariness and tension. The drawn quills made an ugly heap on the stones beside him, clotted with blood and pus. Aracco wiped the thorn-pullers clean and tucked them into his belt.

"Wait a little more," he whispered to the leopard as he retreated toward his fire. He poured the warm water and comfrey into the folds of his headcloth and, creeping back, laid it against the cloud leopard's jaw. Again she jerked back, growling.

"It will take out the pain," he whispered hurriedly.

141

"The Osi taught us." The leopard blinked at him and let him set the poultice, but her tail was lashing. When the cloth in his hands grew chill, Aracco put it down. Too tired now to be afraid, he turned away and crawled back to the fire.

"Are you hungry, my sister?" he asked over his shoulder. Unwinding the cheese cloth, he tossed the rabbit carcass to the leopard and wrapped himself in his cloak. The firelight faded. He heard the sounds of bones cracking as the leopard ate and, later, the soft sound of her paws whispering on stones as she paced away. Thankful for his mother's dreams and the healing skills she had taught him, Aracco fell asleep.

In the morning, he woke abruptly. Shaking off the fear that had clouded his dreams, he scanned the riverbed. The only signs of the leopard were a few scattered bones on the sand and the pile of quills. The stream murmured reassuringly. He looked up at the mountains, brilliant now with sunlight. *How hard,* he wondered, *will it be to climb them? How will I choose a route among so many cliffs of stone? Is there really a road to Terenger, as the old men say? A road that tunnels through the mountains?* At the thought of the tunnel, Aracco shivered. He had no wish to burrow in the darkness like a mole. Far better, he thought, to scale the cliffs in sunlight.

He ate a summerfruit, wondering how many days it would take to reach Terenger. He had waybread, fruit, and a full flask of water, but no meat now, and little patience left for hunting. Counting back, he realized five days had passed since he left Meged. Today, then, was the day of the contest. He balled up his cloak and stuffed it in his pack.

Are my mother's words true? he wondered, uncertain of his path. *Have I run away—like Gemmel?* Picking up a stone, he hurled it toward the river. Seri, Chak, and Nago would match their skills today, striving for the mark of first apprentice.

Maybe I should be there too, he thought. *Gemmel, at least, knew what he was choosing. When I reach Terenger, what then? Return home and be a smith's apprentice? Even if I carry gold and honor back to Meged, that will not tell me what my gift might be.*

He thought about the paths he could follow when his apprenticeship was served. If he gained some skill with words, he might become a trader. Or leave the guild and be a goldclimber. More choices tumbled through his mind. Live with his Dahiri kin. Become a herder. Join a riverboat crew. They made him angry. For none of them, not even climbing, did he feel the strong desire that Seri and his father had for working gold. Just this urge to wander. And what kind of path was that?

He flung stones into the river until his arm was aching. Finding still no answer, he put on his pack, clambered out of the riverbed, and set off through the trees. Before long he came to the upper edge of the forest. In front of him, open meadows sloped up toward the peaks of the mountains. Feeling very small, he hesitated in the shadow of the trees. He felt as if sharp eyes were watching him. Eirocs! In the time since the leopard had appeared at his fire, he had forgotten all about them. Carefully, he scanned the sky. Once he left the forest, he would be easy prey for the giant death hawks.

The sky appeared empty of wings. *Maybe the eirocs are all at the goldcliffs,* he thought hopefully. He grasped that thought, trying to shake off his uneasiness. His only shelter while he crossed the meadows would be in small, scattered groves of firs. He measured the distance between groves with his eyes and shuddered. Too far to run from a swooping eiroc, that was certain.

Aracco gazed up at the mountains, seeking courage. Beyond them lay Terenger. He had sworn to find it. And, by Barak, he would rather climb the mountains than be confined, safe in Meged! Glancing over his shoulder, with a word of thanks to the forest that had sheltered him, he left it behind.

The meadows were lush after the dusty colors of the forest. Bright white and yellow flowers sprang out of the turf, but Aracco was too anxious to pay them much heed. Moving in a zigzag course, he crossed from one clump of firs to the next, pausing each time to glance up at the sky.

There was still no sign of eirocs. Aracco began to feel foolish. *Am I a shrewmouse,* he thought, *scurrying from one tunnel to the next?* At last he left the safety of the trees and headed straight across the meadow toward a narrow, shadowed canyon. On one of his zigzags, he had noticed that the canyon seemed to angle toward a saddle lying low between two peaks. It seemed as good a place to climb as any. As he drew near the canyon, the carpet of flowers around him gave way to purple-blossomed rhoden bushes. Among the bushes just ahead, he saw a pathway of gray stone.

"Barak's truth!" exclaimed Aracco. He hurried forward. The pebbled track climbed steadily toward the narrow canyon he had chosen. Heart pounding, he stepped onto the path. This must be the way the old men had spoken of, the road to Terenger!

Aracco strode swiftly up the track, following it into the shadows of the canyon. The canyon walls were steep, carved of the same dull gray stone. Gullies in the cliffs held fading patches of snow. Slides had dumped broken rock across the pathway, but Aracco scrambled surefooted over the boulders. Now he had a clear path to follow, the wizards' road across the mountains! Excitement pulsed inside him. He hurried up through the rising morning, eager to stand on top of the saddle and look down at Terenger.

It was almost silent in the canyon. He heard only the wind and the scuffing sound of his soft leather boots.

"Ker-raaaaa!" The harsh scream of a bird split the silence. Aracco dove into the space between two boulders and flattened himself against the ground. "Ker-aaa!" The cry was fainter this time. He twisted in his hiding place, gazing up at the sunlit peaks. A bird of prey soared dark against the sky. He thought it was too small to be an eiroc, but he could not stop shaking. His bare arms tingled in the cold air. Taking off his pack, he pulled out his felt jacket. When he finished buttoning it and had put on his pack again, he looked up at the sky. The hawk—if it was a hawk—had wheeled out of sight. Aracco crawled into the open. He scurried up the path, his chilled hands tucked under his arms and his heart still thumping.

Not long after, he rounded a bend in the canyon and stopped abruptly. He heard the blood singing in his ears. Ahead of him the path disappeared beneath an avalanche of jumbled boulders. Above the chaos of fallen stone, the sheer sides of the saddle loomed against a deep blue sky.

Terenger! he thought. *It must be just across the saddle. All I have to do is scale this cliff. With the River's grace I'll be in Terenger by nightfall!* He studied the cliff, looking for a route to climb. Above the boulders of the slide, dark patches caught his eye. It looked as if the gray cliff had been scarred by lightning. Around the black patches the rock was strangely shaped; long straight cracks that met and sharply changed direction. Puzzled, Aracco stared at the mottled cliff and even angles. Suddenly he realized what it was.

"A keystone!" he exclaimed, letting out a low whistle. "So it's true." The Osi *had* carved a tunnel through the mountains. The black patches were not stone, but dark holes below the buried archway. Looking up at them, Aracco shivered. He rubbed sweaty hands on his leggings, relieved that the tunnel was blocked. River's blessing! He would rather climb sunlit rock than burrow in the dark. Scaling the cliff seemed far wiser than stumbling lightless through an ancient tunnel.

Aracco scanned the cliff once more and began scrambling over the boulders. To the left of the keystone was a route that looked good. He was eager to feel firm stone beneath his fingers.

A little past midday, he reached the foot of the cliff. He clambered onto one of the boulders that lay against it. Pulling the waybread out of his pack, he looked up at the steep route overhead. He climbed it with his eyes, along a deep crack to a narrow ledge halfway up. Good. He could rest there and catch breath for the next pitch.

Above the ledge was a sloping face of rock. He could see few handholds. That face would be hardest to climb. Tearing off a piece of bread, Aracco grinned. Balancing. The hardest way of climbing and the best. A climber knew who he was then, knew the slightest change of tension in each and every muscle. Chewing on the bread, he considered the rest of his route. Above the sloping face was another ledge where he could rest before climbing the last pitch. There the cliff was steeper, but even from here he could see cracks and shallow ledges. That looked easy enough. He brushed off the crumbs, swallowed some water from his flask, and put his pack on. Stepping to the cliff, he stretched out his hand for the first hold.

The crack was a good one. Aracco jammed his right foot into it, while his fingers closed on a nubbin of stone. He pulled his other leg up, molding his foot to fill the crack. With his free hand, he reached higher. Aracco's hand slid into the next hold, touching the rock like a smith caressing polished gold. Inching steadily upward, shaping his hands and feet to fit the rock, he felt solid as the cliff itself. No chance of him peeling off, like Valaren. . . .

Aracco's foot twisted in the crack. He closed his eyes, fighting the pain that formed around an image of his friend lying dead in the quarry. Fury rushed in, smothering his pain. *If not for Nago, Valaren would still be alive, vying for the mark of first apprentice. And I would be there too.* He leaned away from the cliff, ignoring the cramp in his foot, and thought about the contest. It was just past midday. Were they melding now? Nago would do well in that skill test, curse him!

I hope Seri wins! thought Aracco. *That will make Nago's feathers droop!* He clung to the cliff, imagining her hands matching two edges of gold, and tried to calm himself. Like the smith who shaped hot gold, a climber needed total attention to his task. Seri would give the contest that attention, held as completely in her crafting as by the music when she danced.

148

My father is right, he thought, remembering the longing on Seri's face that day he'd climbed the Beak, when they had talked of working in the smithy. *She does have the gift to be a goldsmith.* His mind filled easily with images of Seri. He wanted to repeat his parting words. He wished he had the gift of speaking mind to mind.

"Seri," he said. "I truly hope you win." Saying it aloud to the silent mountains made him feel less angry. Tilting his head back, he looked for his next move.

In rhythm again, he climbed toward the ledge above him, only faintly aware of the blood on his knuckles and his aching feet. Discomfort was as much a part of climbing as the sun's warmth and the cool air on his face.

Aracco pulled himself onto the ledge and crouched down, flexing his hands and rocking on his stiff feet. Although the ledge was wide enough to sit on, it was littered with loose stones. He dared not risk knocking one over the edge. The herders had told him that the noise of falling stones attracted eirocs. With one hand grasping the rock, he turned to look down at the canyon. Beyond its narrow walls, beyond the forest and the rolling tawny hills, lay the Great River. Next summer, by the mastersmith's decree, the First Gift would be cast by the apprentice who won today's contest. Maybe Seri would stand among the smiths and watch her goldwork gift the River. Unless Chak or Nago won.

Nago's good at casting, he thought unwillingly. *Almost as good as Valaren.* He felt a cloud pass overhead. Looking up, alarmed, he saw that the sky was still untarnished.

Taking a few deep breaths, he tried to push away thoughts of the contest. *Seri's had my father's teaching,* he told himself as he stood up. Now for the balancing!

He turned toward the cliff and began to climb the sloping face, his hands pressed against the rough stone. His feet matched the shape of the rock. He flowed upward, pausing only when he reached small nubbins or tiny cracks. It felt like walking in the sky.

The slope grew steeper. Aracco's heart began to pound. Had he judged it rightly? Now there was no crack he could cling to, no hold to meld him to the stone. Only balance and the tenuous bond of his hands and feet kept him on the cliff. He climbed swiftly, ignoring the tightness in his stomach. Sweat clung to his shoulders and spine, held there by his pack. Glancing up, he saw blue sky above the gray rock. Not so far now. Soon he would reach the second ledge. From there it was only a short climb to the saddle. Soon he would look down at Terenger. He grinned and shifted slightly on the rock. His chest filled with pride and, suddenly, Nago's face leered in his mind. He stiffened, and felt his foot slip.

Aracco slid backward, his hands rasping down the rock. *Balance!* he thought. *Find it!* His stomach lurched into his throat. *No!* If he scuffled for a hold he would peel off. He flattened out, trying to be like water flowing over stone. The gray rock seemed to blur before his eyes. He forced himself to lie flat, gritting his teeth against the heat of friction. His palms, scraped raw, burned with pain.

With a shock that jarred his whole body, his feet hit the ledge. Aracco staggered, off balance. Loose rocks, kicked free, clattered down the canyon. His shoulder slammed against the cliff. He grabbed an outcrop, wincing as his raw hands closed around the stone. Desperate, he held on. Swaying on the brink, he listened to his thudding heart. Images flew past his vision. He saw his mother's dark face smiling . . . his father's hands cradling a golden thrush . . . Seri dancing in the guildhall. The canyon seemed to spin around him. He tasted bile and felt his sweat turning cold.

Slowly, his world stopped spinning. Aracco collapsed onto the ledge, sucking in great sobs of air. His body throbbed with scrapes and bruises. He crouched there, waiting for his shoulders to stop shaking. Above his head, a shrill scream rent the air. Shadows blocked the sun. Aracco's head jerked back. A giant bird swooped down on him, its claws outstretched.

151

13

Stunned, Aracco stared up at the eiroc. Its talons were the color of dried blood. He shrank down, cling-ing to the ledge, as the death hawk descended.

Wizards save me, he thought, staring up at glitter-ing black eyes. He felt stupid, frozen stiff with terror. The eiroc's beak was cinder black and curved like a Dahiri sword. He cringed at the thought of being slowly torn apart.

Before the eiroc could strike, Aracco straightened, resolute. He had not just scraped off half his skin to be plucked off the cliff by a bird! Scooping up a loose stone bigger than his fist, he hurled it at the eiroc. The death hawk screeched and wheeled away.

Aracco scrabbled for more stones, grimacing with pain. He wedged himself against the cliff, a large rock ready in his hand. The eiroc hovered overhead, blocking out the sun. The air around it stank. Aracco grit his teeth and watched the rhythm of its wing-beats. He'd be no easy meal.

The eiroc swooped. Aracco's stone glanced off its wing and clattered down the cliff. A foul wind overwhelmed him as the death hawk skidded past. He choked, nearly retching. Soaring up, the eiroc circled down again. Aracco grabbed another rock. Behind him, he heard a whisper on the stone. A black and silver shadow leaped over him and landed on the ledge again, snarling at the eiroc.

Cloud leopard! thought Aracco. *Praise Barak!* While the leopard held the death hawk at bay, he reached into his belt for his slingshot and searched the ledge for stones. Fitting them into the sling, Aracco hurled one stone after another at the giant bird. Gray-brown feathers eddied in the air. The leopard crouched, tail lashing. Screeching angrily, the eiroc winged backward and perched on a spire of rock. Its uneven, piercing cries shivered up Aracco's spine.

The cloud leopard turned toward him. Its ears were back and its tail lashed the cliff. He pressed himself against the cliff again, his fist tightening around a stone. Would he have to fight the leopard too? As the cloud leopard paced closer, he saw its jaw was slightly puffy. Aracco relaxed, letting the stone drop from his throbbing hand. So it *was* the same leopard.

"Thank you, sister," he murmured, as the cloud

leopard brushed past him. Her ears flickered. She padded a little way along the ledge and paused, looking back at him. Aracco followed on aching hands and knees. His ears rang with the eiroc's screams. The noise echoed off the cliff until it sounded like a dozen eirocs. Nervously, he glanced over his shoulder. The huge bird was still perched on the spire, its mud gray wings half furled.

Suddenly the leopard disappeared into a narrow fissure in the cliff. Aracco hesitated, staring into the darkness before him. If he followed, it would swallow him completely. He had no light to push back shadows. The leopard reappeared and made a noise like a mother cat calling kittens. She vanished into the cliff again, but Aracco stood frozen on the ledge. He was uneasily aware of the weight of his pack. He had broader shoulders than a leopard, and with the pack on, could not turn sideways.

What if I get stuck? he thought, shrinking from the thought. *And where will she be leading me?*

The eiroc's cries sharpened. Looking up, Aracco saw two more death hawks overhead. His attacker swooped from its perch. In desperation, Aracco ducked inside the narrow crack.

Before him, the stone floor sloped down steeply. In the dim gray light, he saw the movement of the leopard's tail. She began to move away from him, descending into darkness. Once again, Aracco hesitated. Here, just inside the cliff, he was safe from the eirocs. He could simply wait until they flew away.

His shoulder throbbed, and he realized that he

ached all over. Could he scale the cliff again, battered and discouraged as he was? A climber needed firm belief in his ability to reach the summit. Right now he was anything but certain. Reluctantly, Aracco took off his pack. He looped a shoulder strap around one arm. The leopard had trusted him last night at his fire. Now he would have to trust her.

As he descended, the dim light faded into darkness. Soon he could see nothing. Inching forward, Aracco slid his feet along the stone. He sheltered his head with one hand, while the other gingerly followed the rough stone wall. He could stand, but the fissure was so narrow in places that he had to squeeze through, tugging his pack behind him. The blackness pressed down on him until he stopped short, fighting panic.

When we reach the tunnel, he told himself, *it will not be so dark. The Osi crafted it!*

Clutching that hope, he moved on again. Surely the fissure led to the tunnel. He could hear the whisper of the leopard's footpads just ahead, could feel his heart pounding in his ears. It was cold. Aracco thought longingly of the cloak in his pack, but dared not risk losing sound of the leopard.

His right hand reached suddenly into emptiness. Aracco froze. The air was different here, filled with whispers and echoes that quickly died away. He crouched down, his arms wrapped tight around his knees, listening for the cloud leopard. What now? Had she vanished? What lay before him in the blackness?

With startled relief, he felt her warm breath on his

155

hand. She was below him then. Aracco sat down and searched the stone before him with one foot. Feeling the brink, he swung his legs cautiously over the ledge.

How far down? he wondered, listening to his pounding heart. *Not so far,* he reassured himself, *maybe the height of the cloud leopard's shoulders. Half a fathom.* Putting on his pack, he pushed himself forward, bent his knees, and jumped.

Landing, he rocked on his feet, savoring the taste of satisfaction. He had judged it well and landed well. The stone floor was smooth and cold beneath his feet. He felt triumphant, and the strength of it eclipsed his aching weariness. He had escaped the eirocs and reached the tunnel that would lead him into Terenger!

Then Aracco's satisfaction drained away, leaving his mouth dry. He could see nothing. He closed his eyes, then opened them again to utter blackness. He took a deep breath, to prove to himself he was breathing. Only his heartbeat, breath, and bruises told him he was still alive. He had no sense of anything beyond his body. He wished he had a light, even one of the coals from his fire. He felt trapped and as helpless as he had on the day when Nago shut him in the charcoal storeroom. Was this the tunnel of the wizardfolk? Had all their magic deserted it, leaving only a black hole in the mountains? He had coaxed himself through the fissure with the thought that when he reached the tunnel, it would be better, but there was no hint of light to tell him the shape of the place that he stood in.

Something soft and warm pushed beneath his hand. Aracco's fingers tightened in the leopard's fur and tears sprang into his eyes. "Will you guide me then?" he whispered in the Dahiri tongue. "Can even a night hunter like you see in this darkness?" His words crept along the walls, and for a moment he guessed the shape of the tunnel by sound: curved walls, high roof, and a wide, smooth floor.

Ears and whiskers, he thought, *sound and touch, that is how she finds the way.*

The leopard started forward. Aracco moved with her, his feet uncertain. His footsteps sounded loud in the still air. He closed his eyes and listened. He could hear the whisper of the leopard's padded feet and his own shuffling steps, but beyond that, only silence.

It would be better to have noises, thought Aracco. *Rats, winged mice—anything would be better than this.* There was not even a trickle of water. He thought he might even welcome the screech of an eiroc if it would break the silence. The air felt chill and sluggish on his face. Tasting his own fear, he dug his fingers into the leopard's fur. She answered with a warning rumble deep in her throat. Aracco loosened his grip. He dared not make the leopard angry. He felt cold air creep down his back, and sudden terror curled around his heart. Without her, he was helpless.

Following the leopard, Aracco stumbled toward

the left, then right. Sightless, he could not judge his footsteps. One foot came down hard, jarring his sore body. Then, with the next step, his caution caused him to lurch forward. Each time the distance seemed to vary, the tunnel floor too close or far away. A breeze brushed across his face, bleak and damp. Aracco tightened his grip on the leopard's ruff and knelt down, searching the floor with his right hand. He felt a sharp edge, and then emptiness from which a faint wind rose. The leopard growled softly. Aracco straightened up, his heart thumping. If she lost patience and left him . . .

The thought was so horrible that his mind cast it out, scrabbling for something else to fill its place. He blinked a few times, but the blackness was unaltered. He wondered again how the leopard found her way. Maybe her night eyes found light beyond his vision. Maybe she could hear the shapes of stone.

The leopard's shoulders shifted underneath his hand. Aracco stopped, feeling her tail whisk past him as she curled it around her haunches. A wind from the depths chilled his face again. Leaning down, his fingers found the edge of a fissure. The leopard shook his left hand free. Aracco bit his mouth to keep from crying out. Without her solid warmth beneath his hand, he felt dizzy. He heard her leap and land softly on the other side.

But how far? he thought. *Isn't there a way around?* He groped along the floor toward the wall of the tunnel, then stopped, ashamed. If there were, the leopard would have shown him. She landed at his side again, and nudged him with her nose, making small, encouraging sounds in her throat.

Aracco lay on his stomach and inched forward as far as he dared, reaching across the chasm, his toes melded to the tunnel floor. His fingertips found only air. More than half a fathom then, but how much more? He pushed himself back onto solid ground, brushing moisture from his face. How much more? More than half a fathom, but less than the full leap of a leopard. He heard the leopard crouch beside him, her tail whisking the floor. Aracco froze, listening hard. He heard the breeze in her fur as she leaped, heard her land lightly. *Not far,* he thought. Hearing her meowl, he stood up quickly. *Not far,* he told himself again, wiping his sweating, stinging palms.

He tightened the belt of his pack, slid one foot back, bent his knees, and leaped.

His head spun dizzily. Cold air whizzed past his face. He stretched out his arms, feeling nothing. His belly tightened. *How far?* he thought. *How far?*

The sudden stone beneath his feet took him by surprise. He heard a whimper in the darkness. He stumbled forward, falling to his hands and knees. The pain felt good, solid, real. With a flush of shame, he realized he had made that whimpering sound. The leopard licked his cheek with her warm, rough tongue. Aracco wrapped his arms around her neck and hid his face in her thick fur.

After a moment he stood up, wincing. His landing had jarred all his muscles and set his bruises throbbing. *How much farther?* he wondered. He longed to wrap himself in his cloak and escape the darkness into sleep. Feeling the leopard move beside him, he buried his hand in her fur. They moved forward together through the darkness, Aracco following the pressure of her shoulders around fissures and other unseen dangers. When the leopard stopped again, he stiffened, but felt no wind rising from the tunnel floor. Instead there was a deadness to the air, as if it had met a wall. Reaching out, his fingers met the rough surface of a boulder.

The leopard shook his hand free again and sprang up the rock. Aracco began to climb. The stone felt reassuring. Here he did not need to see, here his hands—sore as they were—could guide him. He wondered how high the roof of the tunnel was, but shook off the thought and concentrated on the rock beneath him. Moving surefooted over the jumbled boulders, he climbed upward. His heartbeat was steady and his breath kept the rhythm of his movements. This he understood, this he could do unguided. When the air overhead closed in, Aracco reached up cautiously and felt rough stone. He measured the distance between the boulder and the tunnel roof with his arm. Sliding over the top of the boulder on his belly, he swung around until his feet found a new footing. He heard the leopard's call below him. Her meowl echoed off the stones, and for a brief moment, he guessed the shapes of the huge rocks that blocked the tunnel. Then the echoes died and he saw only the blackness all around him. Aracco climbed down, holding the remembered image firmly in his mind.

He felt the tunnel floor beneath his feet and staggered, his legs shaking with weariness. The short climb had taxed his remaining strength.

"I need to rest," he whispered to the leopard. The tunnel caught his voice and made it echo.

"Rest . . . rest . . ."

She replied with a coaxing sound from deep inside her throat. He stumbled forward, leaning half his weight upon her shoulders. To his right he felt cold air rising from the tunnel floor. He shivered. The leopard nudged him away from the fissure, pacing onward through the night.

Finally the leopard stopped. Aracco noticed it too late and staggered forward. His shoulder slammed against the tunnel wall. He slid to the ground, groaning. He could hear the leopard curling up beside him. Taking off his pack, he found the rough wool of his cloak and pulled it over his shoulders. He groped for his water flask, drank deeply, then put it back inside his pack and drew the cord. Reaching out, he felt the leopard's fur and stroked her gently.

"Thank you, sister," he whispered. Drawing his aching hand into the shelter of his cloak, he closed his eyes. It felt less dark then; he didn't expect to be able to see with his eyes closed. He knew he should sleep, but he was afraid of dreaming. He thought of eating something, but opening his pack again seemed too much effort. He wished he had some meat to give the leopard.

I'll eat in the morning, he thought, and felt another whimper escape from his mouth. There would be no way of knowing when the morning came. Wrapping his cloak tight around his shoulders, he listened to the steady breathing of the leopard. After a while, the sound lulled him and he dozed, wandering into gentle, sunlit dreams.

Rousing suddenly from sleep, Aracco tensed, listening. Something—some sound—was missing. Slowly, he stretched his hand out toward the leopard. He felt only stone and empty air. He was alone in the black and broken tunnel of the Osi.

Aracco stood up, feeling small and cold. The heavy
darkness pressed against him. He cleared his throat,
meaning to call out to the leopard. Fear stopped him.
What else might his voice call out of the blackness?
The silence, which had been so empty before, now
seemed menacing. He felt surrounded, as if the tunnel walls were closing in. In the smithy he felt confined, but this was worse. Worse even than being
shut inside the smithy's dark storeroom. Needing
movement, he shuffled forward and heard a stone,
loosened by his foot, clatter over an invisible brink
into the depths. He retreated toward his pack and
huddled underneath his cloak.

Where is the leopard? he wondered. *When will she
return?* Staring into the blackness, he shuddered
with sudden apprehension. What if she did not? He

clenched his fists against his rising fear and tried to think of something he could do. Then the darkness would not be so horrible. His mind offered only two small words.

Nothing. Wait.

Anger blazed up inside him, refusing to accept this answer. There must be something! But no thoughts came, and the flame of his anger snuffed itself out under the heavy darkness. Despite his warm cloak, he was shivering. He felt as naked as a journeyman stripped down for the test of skills that marked the passage rites for becoming a smith.

His stomach grumbled. Opening his pack, he groped for food. His fingers found the round smoothness of a summerfruit. Aracco bit through the skin. The sweet, familiar taste rested on his tongue, drawing his thoughts homeward. In his mind he hurried through the streets of Meged, down the river road to where his mother's house was waiting. Opening the door, he stepped inside.

He saw his mother, sorting herbs on the big oak table. He heard his father's voice, praising one of Seri's castings. Envy twisted briefly in his heart, wishing the praise had been for him. Then he saw Seri, kneading bread in the cookery, her face aglow. The vision had a vividness, as if his inner self could really travel, quick as thought, as legend said Osiann did.

But I'm no wizard, thought Aracco, skimming the summerfruit pit across the unseen tunnel floor. *If I were, I'd call Valaren here to keep me company.* His stomach soured and he reached into his pack again, seeking the waybread. His fingers touched cool metal. Slowly, he drew out Valaren's climbing iron, and with it, pain. He raised his arm, wanting to hurl it into the blackness.

Valaren, he raged, *if only you'd been roped. If you had only stopped to think!* In his mind, an unwelcome image formed of Nago clinging to the Beak. Knots tightened in his stomach. Still holding the climbing iron, he lowered his arm. His friend had been quick to the aid of another.

And I was not, Aracco thought. *I was gloating.* Admitting it wrenched him apart, opening the festered wound inside. His buried shame began to fill the tunnel, tearing into him like claws. He gritted his teeth. This time he would not turn away. Alone in the darkness he faced his shame.

May both the River and Valaren forgive me, he thought, choking on a sob. *If I had not relished Nago's fear . . .*

Shakily, he drew a breath, reluctant to go on. Tears were rising, stinging, in his eyes. The relentless truth surged to the surface of his mind.

If I had not, he confessed, *Valaren would still be alive.*

Something broke inside him. Tears washed his face and spilled onto his fingers. He wailed aloud and heard the echoes swell into a hundred voices, all of them his own voice, weeping for Valaren. Sobs shook him, tearing at his stiff and aching muscles. Crouched above the pain, he wept until his tears were nearly gone.

I tried to escape . . . knowing my part . . . in Valaren's death. His stomach twisted with another sob.

"Forgive me, Valaren." He stumbled on the words as more tears came. His gut ached and his ears strained, longing for an answer from his friend. *Where is he now? I wish I had the skill to call him.* His heart reached out, seeking the spirit of his friend. He heard his sobs echo in the tunnel—nothing more.

At last, scoured clean, he huddled underneath his cloak, exhausted. He longed to sleep, but now there *was* something more. He felt a gentle presence in the tunnel, as if Valaren sat beside him, waiting patiently.

Aracco raised his head, staring at the blackness, wondering if the warmth he felt was all illusion. But, after a while, still sensing the presence of Valaren's spirit, he forced himself to face the rest of it. *My blame,* he told his friend. *I tried to place it all on Nago.* He felt the warmth increase, as if Valaren had smiled. Then, choking on each word, he whispered one plea more.

"Nago, forgive me."

Even whispered, the words tasted bad.

Perhaps he isn't all to blame, Aracco thought, *but he's still a scorpion.* He glared at the darkness, daring his friend's spirit to contradict him. And heard a memory of his mother's voice. "Poor child."

Why, by the River, had she said such a thing? Nago was a bully and a cheat and the mastersmith's son. *Why,* he demanded of Valaren, *should I pity him?*

There was no answer. The presence he had felt had faded with the echoes. A sharp longing for light and warmth and comfort ached like hunger deep inside him.

Eat some waybread, he thought. *That will settle it.*

He placed the climbing iron gently in his pack and heard it click against something. Searching with his fingers, he pulled out a round white glow.

Hod's lumestone! He had forgotten all about it. He held it up, his heart pounding. Maybe it would light his way! The lumestone rested on his palm, a small moon reflecting on an earth-brown cloud. Aracco smiled, delighted to see colors. Its soft light drew him in, making it hard to look away. At first he did not try, but sat content, reveling in sight. The waiting question rose again.

Why, he asked the stone, *should I pity Nago?*

In the depths of the lumestone, an image formed. Aracco stared. Hod had said the stone granted visions. Bending closer, he gazed at the image in the stone.

Two figures circled in a cage. Bars of gold surrounded them. Their keeper stood outside. As they turned he saw their faces. Himself and Nago. Snarling at each other. Like two wild beasts. The keeper wore the guildhall seal. The mastersmith.

Both of us, Aracco realized, *are caught in the same*

167

cage. He lowered his hands a little, pondering this. *Is the burden of being the mastersmith's son as heavy to carry as that of my own father's skill? If so, no wonder Nago is so swift to quarrel.*

Slowly, understanding came to him, and with it, a little sympathy for Nago. *He's full of thorns,* Aracco thought, *just like the leopard. He needs a healer.* But would Nago stand still while someone pulled his thorns? Aracco doubted it. Any healer who tried to help Nago would get a face full of claws.

He grimaced at the thought of Nago's taunts. Even now, they stung like fireplant. Daki. Horse hands. Dung hands. Coward.

Aracco let the words run through his mind, over and over, until they finally lost their power. *Poor Nago,* he thought, his rancor toward the other boy diminishing. When he returned home, Nago's insults would trouble him less. He understood now that his enemy was lashing out in pain, like a wounded leopard.

When I return? First I have to get out of this tunnel! He held the lumestone overhead and looked around. Disappointment settled heavy in his stomach. The stone's light was far too faint to guide him. It did not even cast a shadow. Lowering his arm, Aracco hunted through his pack again and found the waybread and his water flask.

At least, he thought, gazing at the lumestone while he ate, *I can see a little.* With the soft glow in his hand, the darkness seemed less frightening. *I will get out,* he vowed. *Somehow. I will find Terenger.*

His hunger satisfied, he cupped the lumestone in both hands. Hod's gift drew his thoughts back toward home. He remembered taking leave; his father's love and his mother's challenge. *What path would I choose,* he wondered, *if I could do it over? This one?* Ruefully, he touched the wisdom of his mother's warning. The mountains were not gentle. He had almost fallen from the cliff, nearly been prey to an eiroc.

And now I'm alone in the dark, he thought.

To escape the chill of that, Aracco stared at the glowing stone. Its light illuminated his hands: broad palms, skin scraped from his fall; short fingers, callused from his work in the smithy. A smith's hands? Despite his wish to please his father, he had little desire to be a smith. A climber's? He loved to climb, but didn't really care about finding the gold. Not like Gemmel did. It was only adventure and the raw stuff of life that drew him to climbing. Would he chafe under the orders of the climbers' guildmaster as he did under Jeron's? It seemed likely. He was not well cast to serve a master.

I want to roam free, he thought, *like the Dahiri. I want to watch birds soar and taste the wind and feel the breath of life beneath my fingers. Perhaps mine are Dahiri hands.* His cousin Segev's hands were as dark as night, strong and slender. *Like my mother's,* he thought, remembering her graceful fingers sorting herbs. He stared at his own blunt hands in the light of the lumestone and shrugged. *I am not Dahiri,* he decided.

Who am I then? The question spilled out of the lumestone, coursing down the lifelines on his palms. He felt it rushing through his veins, arousing all his restlessness. But now he felt no anger. Instead the question stretched out before him, a pathway waiting to be explored. Following it in his mind, he settled back against his pack, under his cloak of Dahiri wool. With the lumestone cradled in his hand, Aracco fell asleep.

He woke to unaltered blackness, but his cheek was damp. A furry weight pressed against him. The leopard's tongue washed his face, a warm, rough poultice.

Aracco laughed, tickled by her barbed tongue and giddy with relief. "Are you a healer, then?" he whispered, remembering the hidden shame that now was gone. "Did you know I needed one?" He raised the lumestone and saw two round moons reflected in the leopard's eyes.

"May I call you Kali?" he asked humbly. "You are as wise as my mother." Whatever the leopard's purpose had been, by leaving him alone in the tunnel, she had cleansed many of his inner wounds.

She licked his face again and nudged him to his feet. Aracco put his cloak and the lumestone into his pack, then hoisted it onto his shoulders. Placing his hand on the leopard's ruff, he followed her meekly through the tunnel.

Aracco was stumbling again with weariness by the time he noticed the shadows. Staring ahead, he realized he could see vague shapes in the darkness now. His heart beat faster. Were they nearing the end of the tunnel? Straining his eyes, he picked out the rough edge of a boulder and the deep shadow of a fissure crossing the tunnel floor. He lengthened his stride until he was moving faster than the leopard, tugging at her fur. She growled softly. He rubbed her ear, apologizing.

"We're almost out, Kali!"

Soon he could see well enough to walk alone. He threw his shoulders back, casting off the weight of darkness, and breathed in deeply. The air smelled of sunbaked rocks and trees.

Almost there, he thought, *almost there.* He was surefooted now, his excitement giving him new strength. Soon he would stand in Terenger!

"Hurry, Kali," he urged the leopard, dodging rubble and three narrow fissures. The tunnel curved and opened out. Daylight blazed in his face. Aracco stopped, blinded. He stood blinking until his eyes could bear the light. Before him, the end of the tunnel framed the sky. Aracco started to run. Instantly the leopard sprang in front of him, barring his way. Her ears were flat and she was growling.

Aracco shrank back, startled and afraid. Why had she turned on him now? So close to Terenger? He drew back slowly. The hair on his neck prickled and his hands felt cold.

The leopard chuffed at him, turned and padded forward, then stopped, her tail sweeping dust along the floor. Beyond her front paws lay a jagged chasm. Aracco stared at it, trembling. Half a fathom, no more, but staring out at the sky, he would not have seen it.

"Thank you, Kali," he said, grateful. Her ears flickered and she leaped gracefully across the fissure. She sat waiting for him on the other side. At the chasm edge, Aracco bent his knees and sprang. He soared across, landing lightly. A few paces later, he stood in sunlight.

Aracco stood facing the sky. Below him and on either side, the mountains dropped steeply. *Into Terenger!* he thought. *I've crossed the eastern mountains!* Although he was standing in a rocky hollow midway down their slopes, he felt as if he stood upon the highest peak. At his feet, a narrow track descended into lush meadows and a forest of dense green firs. A breeze lifted the scent of trees to greet him. He took deep breaths of the moist, fragrant air. He reveled in it, glad of the warmth on his hair and shoulders. Behind him, the sun was sinking toward the peaks. It was late afternoon. He had been in the tunnel little more than a day. Aracco stretched out his arms, reaching toward the windy sky.

"Terenger!" he shouted. He looked eagerly down the steep, green flanks of the mountains and saw . . .

A sea of fog shimmered in the afternoon light. Only the mountain peaks and high forests pushed above the clouds. Aracco dropped his arms to his sides, disappointed. The urge to hurry down the track before him faded. Once he left the heights, the forest would surround him. And he knew nothing of what lay below.

The cloud leopard brushed against his legs in passing. He watched her pace away toward the jumbled rocks beside the tunnel. *Don't go!* he thought, but knew he could not hold her. She was a creature of the heights. As he watched her, Aracco felt gratitude well up inside him. Truly, she had returned his gift of healing. His anger and confusion lay behind him in the tunnel like a pile of drawn quills.

"May your feet never falter, Kali," he said softly. She looked back at him, blinking her huge golden eyes. Then she bounded away, ascending the cliffs, until her spotted fur blended with the stones.

Aracco turned again to face the mist. He watched the fog move in shifting patterns. Wisps of gray curled through the trees below. He settled against a sun-warmed boulder. The breeze grew stronger, stirring his hair. It swelled into a wind that bent the tops of the trees and howled among the cliffs. He took his cloak out of his pack and huddled inside it, sitting back on his heels. After a while, he stared harder, blinking twice. The fog—was it thinner now?

Slowly the landscape beneath him emerged, green hills—the most brilliant he had ever seen—and the rounded tops of trees. Aracco watched amazed as the tattering fog revealed a vast blue sea. His father had been right. There was no end to it, the sea went on forever.

His gaze came slowly toward the land. Far below him, its outline sharp against the sunlit ocean, a pinnacle of stone jutted up from the water. In its shadow lay a sheltered harbor. Narrowing his eyes, he could just make out the shapes of fishing boats. He saw a cluster of houses dappling the shore, the tiny brown roofs of a village. Aracco sprang to his feet.

Between the houses were gleaming narrow ribbons. They glinted like sungold in the hand of a climber. They shone like a finely polished cup washed clean of powdered clay. The streets of Terenger! They were true color, he was certain of it.

"Gold!" he shouted, flushing a gather of birds from the meadows. He leaned forward, letting his cloak stream out behind him in the wind. Now he cared little who had won the contest. In a day or two, he would stand on golden streets. What were the sea people of Terenger like, that they walked on gold?

And if gold is so common that they pave the streets with it, he thought, *it must be everywhere, ready to be quarried. I've found gold enough to gift the River for a dozen years!* He imagined his return to Meged, dusty as a goldclimber, bearing a pack full of gold from Terenger.

We will feast in the guildhall then, no longer fearing the threat to the goldcliffs.

For a moment his spirits sank, remembering the

eirocs. How would he return over the mountains? Weighted down with gold, he would be easy prey. Was there some other way?

Valaren's words echoed in his mind: "I would like to find a way there. And I would like to travel on the sea." His gaze returned to the boats in the harbor. He had proved his vow and found the streets of Terenger. Perhaps Valaren's second dream would guide him home.

Aracco slung his pack across his shoulders.

"It's true, Valaren," he shouted to the wind. "In Terenger the streets are gold!" Eager now, he plunged down the track into the shelter of the forest.

Two days later, in the twilight before dawn, Aracco came out of the forest. Everything he had seen on the steep trail down from the mountains told him he was in another land. The trail had led him down through thick, mossy forests where the earth was moist and springy. Countless streams tumbled past, plunging down cliffs in sheets of mist. He saw few birds, but heard them singing all around him.

Once, a bushy animal a little smaller than a fox had crossed his path. Each had paused, considering the other. The animal's bright eyes were circled by a mask of black. White fur fanned across its forehead. It sniffed the air with a pointed muzzle, then trotted off into the forest. Aracco wandered on, delighted.

Now he crossed low green hills where sheep were grazing unattended. Long-legged birds stalked through the grass, their white crests bobbing with each awkward stride. Everything was still. Even the birdsongs of early morning were muted by the ever-present fog. Aracco felt its moisture on his face. It hung around him like a cloak, muffling his footsteps. He reached the top of another low hill and paused, his heart pounding. Before him stood the fishing village. It was just past dawn.

He sprang forward, eager to touch gold.

When he reached the outskirts of the village, he saw the fog hanging in gray veils around the high, peaked roofs. Aracco stared. Through the mist, the faces of carved beasts peered out at him. From the rooflines, their wooden eyes seemed to be watching him. He shivered. In the village everything was quiet. Not a single dog had come to greet him. Was everyone asleep? Or was the village empty?

He paused and looked around. He saw a fishing net piled untidily against the nearest house. On a peg beside the door hung a wool hat, damp with fog. A rush broom leaned against one doorpost. Like the rooflines, the doorposts were carved with watchful faces. And around the doorpost guardians, set into the wood, glowed deep red stones. Looking up, he saw a curl of smoke rising from the chimney.

Asleep then. After all, it was still very early.

He crept forward, past the watchful totems. Ahead he saw a gleam—the streets! Aracco lengthened his stride, but did not run. He had no wish to wake the dwellers in this eerie place.

Ten paces more and he walked on gold. His heart pounded as if he had been running. Beneath his feet the paving stones shone like sunlight. He stood triumphant.

He bent down to touch the golden street and paused, half-crouched, frowning. Bending lower, he pried loose one of the shining stones. Holding it, he felt a hammer blow inside that made him close his eyes, blotting out the gold. He took a deep breath and opened them again. The stone still looked and felt the same. Speckled, grainy, rough.

False gold, thought Aracco bitterly. *And I'm a fool!* He hurled the stone away. It shattered. True gold would have sung out, ringing.

Aracco staggered through the sleeping village in a daze. Past the carved faces, past the blood-red stones embedded in the doorposts. The brilliance of the golden streets was blinding now. Shielding his eyes, he sought a way out, a place to hide his disappointment and his shame.

When his feet found the comforting dull color of packed earth again, he wandered on, not caring where this path might lead. He had failed, although he stood in Terenger at last. As he walked, the day grew brighter through the fog, but his spirit felt no warmth.

His footsteps echoed with a sudden hollow sound. Aracco stopped, blinking. He stood on a bridge that spanned a rushy stream. Ahead of him, the road crossed the edge of the sea plain, following the curve of the harbor. The fog pulled back a little, revealing the cliffs of the pinnacle.

Aracco sank down onto the low wooden railing of the bridge.

What now? he wondered dully. Nothing seemed to matter very much, although he felt a painful longing to be home. But how could he return? How could he stand before all of Meged and say there was no gold in Terenger?

Where will we get our gold? The anxious question, which had been asked in the guildhall after the climbers arrived with their tale of eirocs attacking the goldcliffs, echoed in his mind. The answer he had offered was to seek the streets of Terenger.

Well, now I've found them, thought Aracco, *and done no good by it.* He remembered the gloom that hung over the smithy. How much worse it would be when he returned. When all the climbers left the cliffs, the smiths would falter. They would work on until the gold was gone, but there would be no joy in Meged. He imagined his father's face, and Seri's, empty of the pleasure they found in working gold. Like Valaren's face, when his life was gone from it. One by one the hammers would fall silent, and the smiths would leave, seeking work in other halls. Meged would be lifeless too.

I can't go home, he thought, dreading the hopeless faces that would greet him when he said there were no streets of gold. Then he shrugged. *Anyway, I can't get home.* Even if he could pass through the tunnel, there would still be eirocs on the other side. Aracco shuddered. No, he couldn't cross the mountains a second time.

He gazed at the black pinnacle rising from the tip of the peninsula that formed the bay. Beyond it lay the sea. Was there some other way? Below its cliffs, the harbor was emerging from the fog. A fishing boat rocked at anchor, its red sail furled.

Aracco straightened up a little. Red sails, like on a wizard's boat. Were there wizards here in Terenger? *Osiann's eyes!* he thought. *What about the wizards?* Surely they would have the power to subdue the eirocs. Had anyone asked them? He thought back to the day of Seri's passage rites. The climbers had spoken of leaving the cliffs. The smiths had talked of Terenger. No one had even mentioned the Osi. But why not ask their aid?

I could go, he thought, *and seek the wizards' city. Perhaps there is a way. We would have gold again if we knew how to drive the eirocs from the cliffs. I could ask the wizards.* He sat up tall, looking at the sea, as this idea began to cheer him.

Far better, he thought, to seek an unknown path than go home to the smithy defeated and, empty-handed, tell his father that he did not want to be a smith. He could not bear to face the disappointment in his father's eyes.

Would he, in truth, be disappointed? Aracco pondered this, gazing at the sullen water in the shadow of the cliffs. A pale ray of sunlight touched the fishing boat's red sail. Would he be? His thoughts took him swiftly to the guildhall in Meged.

Slowly, in his mind, he turned to face his father. Aracco saw him, sitting in the guildhall, as calm as he had been when Seri was apprenticed. And smiling, with all the warmth that he had given to his parting words. "Go with the River's grace," his father had said, "on whatever path you follow."

Aracco's spirit soared, as if a heavy load had fallen from his shoulders. He had always been sure that his father wanted him to be a smith, but he had never asked if it were so. Now he could see his cage was largely of his own crafting. He tried to remember, and could not, a time when his father had demanded of him that he be a smith. It had been Aracco's own choice to become an apprentice, a way he thought to please his father. *My father will gladly let me choose my own path,* he realized. *And I am not a smith!*

The walls of the guildhall fell away. He sat on the bridge again—in Terenger. He heard sounds behind him in the village now. Children called to one another, and men were whistling their way toward the harbor.

The sun emerged. In the new light, he saw again his vision in the lumestone. The bars of his golden cage lay shattered. He still had his apprenticeship to serve, but when it was finished, he could take any path he chose to follow.

And my father's blessing will go with me.

Lighthearted now, Aracco sprang to his feet, turning toward the harbor. Was there a seaward path to the wizards' city? Perhaps these fisher people knew the way. He had given his word to Jeron to return, but he wanted to bring home more than just a shattered dream.

Aracco crossed the bridge and set off toward the harbor with eager strides. He thought of his father, whose love was as steady as his hand on the hammer. Of Seri, who truly had a gift for working gold. And of his friend Valaren, who had dreamed of traveling on the sea.

I will go, Aracco thought, *and seek my own gift on the journey. I will find the wizards' city.* Ahead, he saw a bright-winged boat sail out across the sunlit sea.

Nancy Luenn had the original idea for Goldclimbers one summer in college when she was working for the U. S. Forest Service in southern Oregon. To write the book, she read about goldsmithing in ancient Greece and South America, visited the metalworking lab at the University of Washington, and consulted with friends who are climbers. Her favorite part of writing the book was creating the world in which it takes place.

As a child, Nancy created worlds inhabited by plastic zoo animals and paper mice. She drew blueprints of the castle she wanted to live in and pictures of the horses she wanted to ride. In high school, she kept a journal and painted pictures of rock stars and imaginary worlds.

In college, Nancy Luenn studied art and educa-

183

tion. She kayaked on whitewater rivers, learned to rock climb and ski, and lived in a tipi for a year. In her last year at school she began writing children's books.

Nancy Luenn now lives in Olympia, Washington. She is the author of *Nessa's Fish*, *Unicorn Crossing*, and *Arctic Unicorn* for Atheneum.